S0-ARA-774

**STEEL MET FLESH AND A ROAR OF PAIN ROLLED THROUGH THE NIGHT.**

Ruff heard shouts from the camp as his knife flicked out again and again. The attacking thing stopped and backed away. Then someone lit a torch and the thing turned and fled.

He walked back to the wagon where a frightened Sarah Farmer launched herself into his arms. Two of the soldiers stood there, watching, wanting to know as Sarah wanted to know. They were all unwilling to believe that something not quite human, indestructible, and totally evil was in the badlands.

When Ruff didn't explain, the soldiers walked away and Sarah was left with him, her body still pressed close, her breasts generous and warm against him.

"Please take care of me," she whispered.

Ruff pressed his lips to her forehead, her throat, feeling her tremble beneath the thin nightdress as she returned his kisses. "I intend to," he answered. . . .

## Wild Westerns by Warren T. Longtree

(0451)

☐ RUFF JUSTICE #1: SUDDEN THUNDER     (110285—$2.50)*
☐ RUFF JUSTICE #2: NIGHT OF THE APACHE     (110293—$2.50)*
☐ RUFF JUSTICE #3: BLOOD ON THE MOON     (112256—$2.50)*
☐ RUFF JUSTICE #4: WIDOW CREEK     (114221—$2.50)*
☐ RUFF JUSTICE #5: VALLEY OF GOLDEN TOMBS     (115635—$2.50)*
☐ RUFF JUSTICE #6: THE SPIRIT WOMAN WAR     (117832—$2.50)*
☐ RUFF JUSTICE #7: DARK ANGEL RIDING     (118820—$2.50)*
☐ RUFF JUSTICE #8: THE DEATH OF IRON HORSE     (121449—$2.50)*
☐ RUFF JUSTICE #9: WINDWOLF     (122828—$2.50)*
☐ RUFF JUSTICE #10: SHOSHONE RUN     (123883—$2.50)*
☐ RUFF JUSTICE #11: COMANCHE PEAK     (124901—$2.50)*
☐ RUFF JUSTICE #12: PETTICOAT EXPRESS     (127765—$2.50)*

*Price is $2.95 in Canada

Buy them at your local bookstore or use this convenient coupon for ordering.

**THE NEW AMERICAN LIBRARY, INC.,**
P.O. Box 999, Bergenfield, New Jersey 07621

Please send me the books I have checked above. I am enclosing $_____
(please add $1.00 to this order to cover postage and handling). Send check
or money order—no cash or C.O.D.'s. Prices and numbers are subject to change
without notice.

Name_____

Address_____

City _____ State _____ Zip Code _____

Allow 4-6 weeks for delivery.
This offer is subject to withdrawal without notice.

*RUFF JUSTICE #14:*

# THE STONE WARRIORS

## By
## Warren T. Longtree

A SIGNET BOOK

NEW AMERICAN LIBRARY

## PUBLISHER'S NOTE

This novel is a work of fiction. Names, characters, places, and incidents either are the product of the author's imagination or are used fictitiously, and any resemblance to actual persons, living or dead, events, or locales is entirely coincidental.

NAL BOOKS ARE AVAILABLE AT QUANTITY DISCOUNTS WHEN USED TO PROMOTE PRODUCTS OR SERVICES. FOR INFORMATION PLEASE WRITE TO PREMIUM MARKETING DIVISION, NEW AMERICAN LIBRARY, 1633 BROADWAY, NEW YORK, NEW YORK 10019.

Copyright © 1984 by New American Library

All rights reserved

The first chapter of this book appeared in *Power Lode*, the thirteenth volume of this series.

SIGNET TRADEMARK REG. U.S. PAT. OFF. AND FOREIGN COUNTRIES
REGISTERED TRADEMARK—MARCA REGISTRADA
HECHO EN CHICAGO, U.S.A.

SIGNET, SIGNET CLASSIC, MENTOR, PLUME, MERIDIAN and NAL BOOKS are published by New American Library, 1633 Broadway, New York, New York 10019

First Printing, June, 1984

1 2 3 4 5 6 7 8 9

PRINTED IN THE UNITED STATES OF AMERICA

# *RUFF JUSTICE*

He knew the West better than any man alive—a hostile, savage land rife with both violent outlaws and courageous adventurers. But Ruff Justice had a sixth sense that kept him breathing and saw his enemies dead. A scout for the U.S. Cavalry, he was paid to protect the public, and nobody was faster at sniffing out a killer, a crook, a con man—red or white, at close range or far. Anyone on the wrong side of the law would have to reckon with the menace of Ruff's murderously sharp stag-handled bowie knife, with his Colt pistol, and the Spencer rifle he cradled in his arms.

Ruff Justice, gentleman and frontier philosopher—good men respected him, bad men feared him, and women, good and bad, wanted him with all the wildness of the Old West.

# 1

⬥━━━◆━━━⬥

"Bastards! Filthy bastards," Ansel Farmer hissed. They were still coming—the Stone Warriors. Farmer had shinnied up the wind-flagged red cedar to look back down their trail, a trail they had followed for day after interminable day through the Little Missouri badlands.

"Are they back there still?" Tom Keep called up. The man was ashen. The hole in his leg wasn't healing properly.

"Yes." Farmer hung his head with despair. They were there; they would always be there. Until they had killed every last one of Farmer's group.

"Oh, God," Keep moaned, his features carved with anguish. He looked skyward into the brilliant Dakota sun. "God damn them! What do they want?"

The boy stood beside Keep. The kid was only sixteen, but he was taller than Keep, and now, as he placed an arm around the injured man, he appeared stronger and older.

Hell, Farmer thought with something approaching astonishment, he was stronger than Keep. Maybe stronger than Farmer himself. And that was something, when a man's son grew taller than he was, when he showed a strength sufficient to see him through in a man's world.

If his son, Andrew Jackson Farmer, ever got the chance to have a man's life.

Farmer looked out across the oak- and ash-stippled badlands again. He could see them distinctly. A patch of red and of blue—a blanket or a daubed war horse. They never got near enough for a rifle shot, however. Not for a good shot, though Farmer and his son, Keep, Dougherty, MacDonald, and Samuels had wasted a hundred rounds of ammunition on the Stone Warriors, trying to keep them off their back trail.

It hadn't worked worth a damn. They were still coming.

"Pa, we'd better get moving!"

"Yeah." Farmer started down the red cedar. He slipped, tore a gash in his forearm, and landed roughly. The boy helped him up.

"There many of them?" the kid wanted to know.

"Twelve. Same as always, Andy. Just the twelve of them."

"That can't be, Pa. I got one. I know I did. Day before yesterday. And MacDonald—he got one back at the crossing, remember?"

"They're still there, Andy. There's still twelve."

"For Christ's sake!" Tom Keep shouted. "Let's get moving."

"Take it easy, Tom."

Keep sat his horse unsteadily. Blood seeped through his pant leg, staining his jeans to a dark maroon. His face was waxen. He would never make it to Lode. Maybe none of them would.

There had been six of them, plus the old Arik, when they started. Now they were reduced to Farmer, the kid, and the badly wounded Tom Keep.

"We won't make it, Pa, not unless we unburden these animals. They're wore down."

Farmer looked at his own blue roan and nodded. The kid was right again. "Tom?"

"I'm damned if I'll leave my gold. Damned if I will! What's it all for, Ansel, if we get back without the gold?"

"It's the only way." Ansel Farmer nodded across the badlands. "They don't care about gold. Don't even know what it is, likely. Ignorant as can be."

"Then you leave your gold, Ansel Farmer. Damned if I will."

"Andy?"

"I already told you what I thought, Pa."

"Half of the gold's yours. Enough to get you started in anything you like."

"Won't do me no good dead," Andy said with a grin. Already he was untying the sacks of dust from his long-legged Appaloosa pony.

"Just hurry up," Keep said. He was clutching his leg with both hands. Blood continued to flow from it, to flow heavily.

Ansel Farmer and the boy hid their gold in a clump of yellow-gray boulders near a lightning-struck, ancient oak. Tom Keep didn't even watch them. His eyes were open, but he wasn't seeing much of anything.

"He won't be able to keep up with us, Pa," Andy Farmer whispered to his father as they crumbled broken rock into the narrow fissure where the eleven sacks of gold dust were hidden.

"No." Farmer shook his head. "He'll never make it with that load his horse is carrying."

"It's damned near murder to let him keep that gold with him."

"You want to take it away from him, son?"

"No." Andy Farmer looked at the wounded man, a

man they had lived with, worked with, shared fire with for eight long months. "No, Pa. I couldn't do that."

"Nor could I."

Keep was looking at them now as they clambered down out of the rocks. The eyes were narrow, filled with pain and suspicion.

"Dammit," Keep hissed, "let's get moving, Ansel."

"Yes." Farmer looked down the long, flood-scoured white gorge behind them. He couldn't see them now, but they were back there. They were Stone Warriors and they would not stop—nor could they be stopped.

That was what the old Arik had told them. "Nothing kills Stone Warriors. You are mad to go to their land to search for gold. All the men they see die. All the men. Ask those who know."

"Who are they?" Farmer had asked across the tiny fire, but the old Arik had shaken his head. He did not know."

"Sioux? Are they Sioux? Some ghost-dancer clan? Something like that?"

"Stone Warriors. If you go to their land, you will not come back. No one will. Ask those who know."

But the Arik had agreed to be their guide into the badlands of western Dakota, to lead them into that tangle of gorges and gullies and weather-scoured hills along the Little Missouri. Three sacks of tobacco and a new Henry rifle had been enough to convince the old man.

Now he was dead. The Stone Warriors had done it. As they had killed Dougherty and MacDonald and Samuels.

The three rode up the long, dry canyon, the super-heated wind moaning in the sparse stand of aspen—sere and gray compared to the high Colorado forests. That was Farmer's home, Colorado, and he longed for it now.

Keep's horse was lagging. They climbed a sandy

draw and the animal sank to its knees. The burden was too much.

"Tom, you've got to unload."

"You go to hell!" the man flared up.

"You'll never keep up."

"Then go ahead without me—go ahead, damn you!"

The boy's eyes were on Farmer, questioning. Farmer shook his head. No, they couldn't leave him. Ansel looked back down the trail again, seeing nothing now but the dusty haze stirred up by the approaching riders. The bottom was soft; he couldn't hear their horses or see them. There was only the dust—and a knowledge beyond the senses.

"Damn you, Tom Keep," Farmer muttered. He swung down from his roan and got Keep's gelding by the bridle, leading it up out of the sandy wash. It stood quivering, foam flecking its flanks.

Ahead of them now the country flattened, smoothed, the long plains beginning. Dry yellow, endless, the Dakota prairie stretching out toward the Knife River and then the Missouri, Fort Lincoln, and safety.

It was a long way, a hell of a long way.

The empty land passed beneath their horses' hooves; the sun was a white-hot hole in a blue-crystal sky burning shoulders and necks, blistering hands. Farmer's horse stumbled and he jerked its head up, cursing. The roan was weary as well. He patted the animal's neck, looking back across his shoulder, knowing what he would see, seeing it.

Dust rising in a thin, wind-twisted column.

"Why don't they quit? Why don't they give it up?" Anguish tugged down at the corners of Farmer's mouth. In anger, in frustration, he pulled his .44-40 Henry from his saddle boot and fired six rounds at the distant dust.

"Pa?" The boy was looking at him oddly.

Farmer could smell the gunsmoke, feel the hot metal

in his hands. He wiped the sweat from his eyes and shook his head heavily. "Why don't they leave us alone?"

"Come on, Pa."

They started again, riding eastward, always eastward across the unvarying plains, ignored by and ignoring in turn the scattered buffalo herds, the quick-leaping blur of pronghorn started into motion at their approach.

Keep's horse went down for good half an hour later. The gelding just folded up, unstrung. It went down hard on its neck, unseating Tom Keep, and it lay there, flanks heaving, eyes wide and showing much white.

"Get up, damn you!" Keep tried to yank it up by main strength, and when that failed, he began beating it with his rifle stock. Beating it savagely, brutally. It didn't matter—the horse was already dead.

"Come on, Tom. We've got to keep moving."

"Give me a hand with my dust."

"I'll take you up behind me, Tom, but I'm not taking your dust too."

"It's all I've got in the world," Tom Keep shouted. He had his rifle in his hands still, and for a moment Andy Farmer thought he was going to turn the gun on them.

"Go on, then. . . . I'm not leaving it."

"Tom, be reasonable . . ."

"Pa, they're coming up a lot faster now."

"Tom!"

"Get out of here, you bastard," Keep shouted, and Ansel Farmer just nodded, turning his roan eastward again. When he glanced back, Tom Keep was staggering after them, his gold-dust sacks tied together and slung over his neck.

"He'll never make it," Andy said. "He'll never make it an hour." There was no reply from his father.

They reached the Knife River in late afternoon. Cool, silver-blue, glistening in the sunlight. Andy Farmer swung down from his horse and stumbled to the river's edge to collapse on his belly against the sandy beach. Then he drank, drank until he was saturated with cool, clear water, until his belly was bloated and cramped with the drinking.

He sat up then, wiping back his blond hair, staring through the willows in the direction they had come from. A lone crow sailed through an empty sky, calling. The land had gone suddenly still around him, and Andy didn't like the feel of it. He could no longer hear the cicadas, the frogs along the river.

"We've got to keep moving, Pa," he said, and the older man nodded heavily.

"Just a minute more." He sat on the sand, his head hanging. His horse drank and drank again. The water on its muzzle was like quicksilver in the sunlight when it lifted its head.

Something stark and cold reached out and ran fingers up Andy Farmer's spine. Tiny voices whispered mocking words in his ear.

"Pa!" The horse's head was lifting, turning as it looked with intensity toward the willows behind them. Its ears were pricked with curiosity, its eyes alert.

It saw, it heard, it knew. And so did Andy Farmer. He threw himself sharply to one side as the arrow flew past his face, burying itself in the sand. He grabbed at his holstered Remington pistol, firing three times into the willows, hitting nothing. He saw nothing, heard nothing. The horse yanked at the end of its tether, but Andy held it tight. His father's horse had gone galloping down the riverbank, stepping on its reins, tossing its head angrily.

"Pa!"

An arrow had gone all the way through Ansel Farmer's neck. Blood purpled the gray sand beneath him. Already the flies were coming.

"Pa?" Andy shook his father's shoulder, knowing it could do no good. Still he was unwilling to let him die, to admit that death could strike that close to him.

He drew away then, his teeth grinding together. He emptied his pistol into the willows, yanked his rifle from his saddle boot, and emptied that as well.

The shots echoed away, smothered by the empty day. The river ran slowly into the distances.

Andrew Jackson Farmer, aged sixteen, swung up into the saddle and headed out across the Knife River, while behind him the Stone Warriors emerged from the brush to do their work on his father's body.

Reaching the far side, Andy rode into the brush, circled back toward the river, and got shakily down. He peered out across the mirror-bright river toward the far shore, knowing what he would see. The old Arik had told them what the Stone Warriors did to their enemies' bodies.

"Every bone. They must break every bone. Some say they do this so that the ghost cannot fight them again. They think they themselves come back from the grave. Maybe so," the old Indian had said, considering it thoughtfully.

Now Andy, his heart pumping wildly, watched them destroy his father's remains. Huge men, giants really, using logs and stones picked up along the river. He could see their arms raised overhead, hear the grunts of effort clearly as they smashed their tools down against Ansel Farmer's body.

They didn't speak; they never spoke, someone had said. They just battered the dead body, pulping and crushing it. Andy counted them. Twelve. His father had been right about that. There were still twelve of them—no matter that two of them had been killed back down the trail. . . . Andy wiped the sweat from his eyes and sighted down the long blue barrel of the Henry repeater he held.

He settled the bead sight into the notch, centered it on the heart of a Stone Warrior, and squeezed off.

Rapidly he levered in a fresh round, already knowing that the first shot had missed to the right. The thing turned slowly toward him, its mouth gaping open in a silent bellow, and Andy shot him again, seeing the Stone Warrior stagger backward as the .44-40 slug tagged him high on the chest.

The Stone Warriors ran to the willows where their horses were concealed, Andy's bullets pursuing them. A second warrior went down, pitching forward on his face to lie there unmoving.

"Two of them," Andy thought. "Two of the bastards."

He scrambled to his feet and leapt for his saddle, turning his horse out of there. The Stone Warriors were splashing across the river now, riding low across the withers of their ponies, waving their bows overhead.

Andy had a last glimpse of them before he reentered the willows and rode hell for it toward the open plains beyond. He had a last glimpse, and he counted them as they rode across the river, silent, implacable. There were twelve of them. Twelve. And not a sign of an injured man on the far bank. Only his father's broken, savaged body.

Andy felt the sob well up in his throat, a sob of futility and confusion. He looked at the Henry rifle in his hand, then flung it violently away, jamming his heels into the flanks of the big horse he rode.

Ahead lay the long plains, the distant Fort Lincoln, and maybe, if a man rode far enough, fast enough, he could escape the death and the madness of the Stone Warriors.

# 2

— · —— · ——

Rachel yawned and blinked away the sleep from her eyes. She stretched her long coppery arms, rolling onto her side. The man in the doorway was naked. Tall, lean, his hair dark and as long as Rachel's own, curling down past his shoulders.

He faced away from her, watching the copper and fire of a dawn sky. Dove winged low above the river, and somewhere far, far away a coyote yelped for a moment and then was silent.

"You are up so early," the gypsy girl said.

Ruff Justice turned toward her. "Yes." He was smiling, his eyes traveling over the sleek lines of her body. Her legs were outlined by the blue sheet. Her breasts were free, unrestrained and inviting, dark-nippled. Her dark eyes shined as Ruff crossed the gypsy wagon to sit down beside her, his hand stroking her black, black hair.

"I've got to pull out this morning, Rachel, you know that."

"Why?" She decided to pout for a while to see if it changed Ruff's mind. Her full lower lip protruded a little and she turned her eyes down.

"I've got to get back to the fort. You know that."

"Why? You don't have to do nothing. You're not a soldier."

"I've got to go." Ruff bent his head to her breast and kissed it teasingly. He could feel her pulse increasing beneath his lips. "Jocko's coming back anyway."

"Jocko can go to hell, too," Rachel exploded. "Who in hell is Jocko?"

"Whoever he is, he thinks he's your boyfriend."

"And you wouldn't fight for me? I'm not so good?"

"I'd fight for you, darlin'," Ruff Justice said. "If I had to. Do I have to?"

She tossed the sheet aside and stretched her hands out toward Ruff. Her fingers wriggled with impatience. Her eyes, bright with emotion, positively shone with eager anticipation as Ruff rolled to her, his thigh meeting hers, his mouth smothering her mouth. Her hands joined behind his waist and drew him more tightly to her as her thighs spread and lifted and Rachel settled Justice between her legs.

Ruff entered her slowly. Looking down, he could see the pleasured smile on her lips. Her eyes were open but unfocused, and as he settled against her, his pelvis meeting hers, she began to murmur gently.

Ruff kissed her breasts, one and then the other, lingering at the taut nipples, running his tongue slowly around them as Rachel began to lift her hips with more emphasis to thrust against him, to sway from side to side.

Her hand stretched out, found his head, and brought it to her mouth. Her kiss was fiery, wet, her tongue darting in and out. The murmuring sounds had become a deeply pleasured moan. Rachel's hands slid down his spine and gripped his buttocks tightly, holding him against her as she gasped and pitched convulsively.

"Ruffin Justice, you are bad. Very bad," she said

breathily, speaking in an oddly rhythmic way. Her hand went behind Ruff now, searching for him, finding herself where he entered her.

Ruff Justice shifted then, getting up onto his knees. He leaned back, smiling. Rachel was wet now, very wet, quivering inside. Her dark hair was spread across her blue pillow. Her hands found him again, touching his shaft as, on his knees, he moved slowly forward and back again, seeing the deep pleasure in her eyes, feeling the touch of her flesh, her urging fingers.

Then he could wait no longer and he reached a sudden hard climax, Rachel's fingers still clutching at him, trying to draw him in still more as she, too, reached her climax, on and on until he went forward to lie against her, to kiss her throat, her chin, eyes, shoulder, and ear.

It was peaceful, still, silent in the gypsy wagon. Outside, the sun painted dazzling patterns on the Missouri, filled the gaps between the branches of the cottonwoods with liquid gold, hot and brilliant. Inside, Ruff had Rachel in his arms. She breathed softly, contentedly.

The door burst open and the big, black bearded man bellowed with rage. "No! Damn you. You're a dead man, Ruff Justice."

Rachel was suddenly sitting upright, her black eyes terror-struck, angry. "Get out, Jocko! Out!"

"Get out! You are my woman and I catch you with this."

"I am not your woman."

The two glared at each other and then began shouting in a tongue Justice did not know. Ruff paid little attention to them. His eyes were on Jocko, on the big knife he held in his right hand, on his own gun belt hanging across the chair behind the gypsy king.

"You!" Jocko was back to English. "I kill you. I kill you." He didn't have much imagination, but he had a hell of a lot of determination. He was going to kill if he could get away with it.

Rachel screamed and threw herself at Jocko, biting, scratching, clinging to the big man, her teeth flashing and eyes wild. Jocko swatted her aside and she skidded across the wagon's floor to lie curled and still in the corner.

Then he came in, growling, his eyes smoldering, the knife held edge up for a belly cut.

Justice crouched, one foot on the floor, the other on the bed behind him. He held his hands loosely in front of him, ready to try to fend off a slashing attack.

"You've hurt her, Jocko," Ruff said. "You shouldn't have hurt her."

"Go to hell," Jocko muttered. He wouldn't even glance that way; Jocko was no fool. He had lived by the knife, they said, from Romania to Dakota, where the gypsy band had finally run out of freedom. Even they couldn't dupe the Sioux and the warring Cheyenne.

They could not cross the plains, and so they had decided to travel southward to Colorado. The miners in the Rocky Mountain boom towns had a lot of loose gold, they said. They had been awaiting only the return of their "king," Jocko.

Jocko had come a day early to suit Ruff Justice. The gypsy king stood blocky and menacing before Ruff, shutting out the light that bled through the shattered door. A stray beam of sunlight caught the gold earring Jocko wore and turned it to fire.

"This isn't going to do anyone any good," Justice said.

"You have insulted me. It cannot be allowed."

"You'll hang for it."

"I do not think so. There are others for whom I have not hung," Jocko said that quite soberly. He seemed relaxed now, almost indifferent, and some instinct warned Ruff Justice that the gypsy was going to make his move.

He did, with a scream and an upward slash of the knife that would have spilled Ruff's guts all over the floor of the gypsy wagon if Justice hadn't been prepared.

Jocko was quick, incredibly quick for a man of his size, but Ruff had had time to pull away and to slap the knife hand of the gypsy king to one side.

In the same movement Ruff ducked under Jocko's arm and drove a knee up at his groin. The knee hit solidly and Jocko, grunting with pain, staggered against the wall. Already Ruff was past him, to the chair where his gun belt lay.

He whirled, his Colt coming up, in time to see the knife fly out of Jocko's hand, to see the exultant glee in the gypsy's eyes.

It was purely luck, but Jocko must have thought Justice had the reflexes of a cat: he half-ducked and struck out with his gun hand. The barrel of the Colt met the knife blade and both weapons clattered to the floor harmlessly. Justice bent slowly and slowly rose, his gun in his hand. His heart was racing, his hand stung with the pain caused by steel meeting steel. All Jocko saw was a tall, naked man with icy-blue eyes and a Colt revolver.

Jocko's hands went up slowly. "All right. All right. I'll go, Justice."

"No. I'm sorry—not now. It's too late, Jocko."

"Don't shoot me, for Christ's sake, Justice. Please!"

"No." Justice calmly placed the Colt back in its holster, turning his eyes deliberately away from Jocko, who launched himself across the wagon in a new rage.

Ruff stepped to one side, stuck out his foot, and tripped the gypsy, clubbing him on the back of his neck as he went by. Jocko thundered into the wall, his skull meeting it first. A shelf on the wall emptied itself of bric-a-brac, which clattered down over the fallen gypsy.

Ruff stepped back and Jocko rose, his eyes tiny, dark, feral.

"Now I don't stop, Ruff Justice. I don't stop until you're dead."

"Come on, then, Jocko, come on." Ruff backed away a little. Jocko growled again. The man was smiling now, smiling, dammit! The gypsy bunched his fists and moved in toward the lanky scout.

But things were even now, and if Jocko had hurt a man or two in his time, they hadn't been of quite the same caliber as Ruff Justice.

Ruff had his blood up and he was ready. He fired a straight left into Jocko's face, a left the big man hadn't been expecting. It was like a snake striking, and like a striking snake, it hit a lot harder than expected. Jocko's head snapped back on his neck and blood gouted from a damaged nose.

Jocko wiped away the blood with his sleeve and came in again, holding his guard higher. Justice hooked once toward Jocko's right ear, then dropped down to bring the left up into the gut. Jocko paled with pain as the wind was driven out of his lungs.

Abandoning all pretense at science, the gypsy flung himself at Justice, his hands clawing for the eyes, but Ruff had been moving away and he stuck two more jabs of his own into Jocko's face before bringing the right over the top. It landed solidly, flush on the cheekbone, and Jocko's face split open. More blood flowed from his face as his nose started to drain again.

Jocko threw his arms up, trying for cover, but Justice was relentless. Moving in, he cut loose a flurry of rights and lefts, below to the belly, up to the head, and Jocko could only back away in confusion.

They were at the open door and Justice feinted with a left, feinted the right, and then stuck the left into the gypsy's face again. It hit smack on the button, and turned Jocko's knees to rubber; he stumbled backward out the door, falling down the three wooden steps to the ground.

Justice was on top of him already, yanking him to his feet. Other gypsies peered out of their wagons, astonished, cheering—angry, amused gypsies. The tall man was naked. They had come out of Rachel's wagon. Now Jocko was getting the beating of his life—that didn't go down all that badly with some of the gypsy tribe. If Jocko was their king, he was also a bit of a tyrant.

"No, Justice . . ." Jocko was hunched forward, his face buried in his arms. He leaned against the gaudy crimson-and-gold wagon behind him, his lungs fiery, dusty, his mouth dry, his nose broken, his cheek split. All of the wind was out of his sails now. He had had enough.

"No more, Justice!" It was Rachel who called out this time. Leaping from the wagon, she ran to where the two men warily faced each other. "Please, Ruff, no more. Don't hurt Jocko."

"Rachel!" Great tears began to stream down Jocko's cheeks, and he threw his arms around the woman. "I'm sorry, so sorry. But you were bad. You know I'm crazy for you."

"I know it, Jocko, I know."

"Now will you marry me? Now."

"Yes. Yes, my king."

Justice stood aside, a smile on his lips. There was a look in Rachel's eyes he didn't quite get, a look that said, "Leave this to me. It will be better my way."

She was right, he guessed. Ruff's own jaw hurt. His hands were scuffed and bruised. He looked around sharply, realizing that he wasn't alone in the wagon circle. He made a dash for Rachel's wagon and his clothes, leaving the gypsy king and the woman to moan in each other's arms and promise all sorts of promises they never meant to keep.

Justice dressed quickly. Buckskin pants, beaded buckskin shirt, boots, and white hat. He slung his gun belt around his hips, shifting it so that the Colt and opposing bowie knife rode comfortably.

Then he walked to the corner, picked up the big .56 Spencer repeater, and turned toward the door. Jocko was there, his arm around Rachel, his face already badly swollen. Justice tensed slightly.

Their eyes met for just a moment and then Jocko stepped respectfully aside, his gaze shuttling away. Ruff stopped in front of Rachel, who now had a blanket around her. She had a small abrasion on her forehead from being thrown to the floor.

"You sure this is what you want, Rachel? There's other places, other people."

"It is what I want," she said quietly. There was something in her eyes that said it wasn't quite what she wanted—but what she really wanted she couldn't have and she was wise enough to know it.

"Then, luck to you, girl." He lifted her chin and smiled for her. "Treat her right, Jocko, or I'll come looking."

Then Ruff stepped out of the wagon and walked past the gathered gypsies to the river, where his black horse was tethered. They hadn't been foolish enough to try and take that horse.

It was a big one, the biggest Justice had owned for a time. Often the big ones were clumsy, but this black was sixteen hands of pure explosive power combined with grace and quickness. It had quick little feet, with the movements of a cutting horse, although it had never been trained to work cattle.

Ruff slipped the bridle on and buckled the throat latch, patting the horse's sleek neck as he looked into that peculiar face marked with a white blaze and topped by one white ear. On one side of the black's muzzle a dozen pure white whiskers grew from obsidian-black hide. From the head on back, there wasn't a hair that wasn't pure black.

The horse hadn't really been tested yet, but Ruff liked it, liked it for its guts and will to run. It had learned quickly to stand while Justice shot from horseback, learned to work a trail guided only by the pressure of Ruff's knees like a good Cheyenne buffalo pony—which it wasn't; a buffalo pony could have stood in the shade beneath the big gelding's belly.

He saddled the horse, his eyes going to the brush at his back from time to time. He wasn't all that sure that Jocko wouldn't have second thoughts.

When he rode out, it was in a great circle, away from the gypsy camp and the town of Bismarck itself, which was now yawning awake.

Fort Abraham Lincoln lay ahead. Dust rose from the parade ground as mounted troops drilled. The flag hung limply on the pole in the center of the parade. Smoke rose from the cook shack. A fuel party was preparing to go out—six men with a wagon to collect dried buffalo dung, the only prolific fuel on the plains.

The sentry at the gate saluted loosely, smiling as Ruff rode into Fort Lincoln. Ruff waved back. He and Corporal Wolfe had seen some times together.

The colonel's office adjoined the Bachelor Officers' Quarters on one side and the armory on the other. There were three army mounts tied before the commander's office and one civilian animal, a strapping, bald-faced gray.

Justice swung down from the big black and walked up the step to the plankwalk, entering the orderly room beyond.

First Sergeant Mack Pierce, huge, flaccid, red-faced, wheezing, broke into a grin and lifted his bulk from behind his desk.

"Welcome back, Ruffin."

"Hello, Mack. The colonel in?"

"He's in and wishing to see you. Just now he's got a civilian visitor. I'll let him know you're here."

Pierce waddled off into the colonel's office while Justice stood discussing the weather with the corporal of the guard. They had just about exhausted that subject when Mack Pierce got back.

"Colonel would like you to go on in now, Ruffin."

"All right."

"Uh, Ruffin, you might want to dab at your face a mite. You've got some blood under your eye."

Pierce handed Justice a mirror from his desk drawer, and Ruff frowned into it, wiping at the bloody cut under his eye with his white silk scarf.

"The hell with it," he said when the cut refused to stop bleeding. "MacEnroe's seen blood on me before."

"Maybe he has—I thought you might want to look your best."

"Mack . . . ?" Ruff cocked his head suspiciously.

"I don't like to spoil surprises, Ruffin." Pierce chuckled. He lowered himself heavily into his chair, still laughing, and when Pierce laughed, everything moved: chins, great belly, haunches, jowls.

Ruff's eyes narrowed still further and he turned toward the colonel's office. He knocked, was summoned, and went in to find Colonel MacEnroe in his best dress uniform sitting behind his desk, a glass of whiskey in hand. And across the desk in a wooden chair, wearing a soft, shy smile of welcome, a beautiful dark-haired, green-eyed woman.

# 3

Ruff Justice closed the door behind him and stood looking expectantly from the colonel to the young woman. MacEnroe, with a half-frown, rose to introduce them.

"Miss Farmer, this is Ruffin T. Justice, the man I have been telling you about."

"Very pleased," Miss Farmer said, but there wasn't a lot of sincerity in her voice.

"Charmed," Justice said, and that nearly covered it, for she was a charming woman, beautiful and intriguing.

"It is Miss Farmer who may need some help, Ruff. If you got my message . . . ?"

"Yes, sir, I got it," Ruff answered.

"Good." MacEnroe turned to the lady again. "Justice was on leave, you see. Relaxing in town." The colonel managed to say that without grimacing or bursting out laughing—he was getting better.

"I see. You are a civilian, though, Mr. Justice?"

"That's right, I am." Ruff smiled. His eyes were active, studying the lines and curves of the woman beneath the green velvet dress, trying to see more deeply into those green eyes than she would allow.

26

She looked away with embarrassment and, it seemed, a little anger.

"Miss Farmer is in need of some help, Ruff. She's naturally come to us."

"Oh?" Ruff walked to a nearby chair, sat down, crossed his legs, and sat observing the woman. "Nothing serious, I hope."

"Serious enough to me," Sarah Farmer said sincerely. Her eyes met Ruff's for a moment, clashed with his, and then fell away.

"We are expecting the rest of her party momentarily, Ruff," the colonel said, "and then . . ."

The colonel didn't have time to finish that sentence before Mack Pierce appeared again in the doorway and announced the arrival of the other civilians.

"Bring them in, please, Mack."

"Yes, sir."

Half a minute later the introductions started again. Ruff stood to shake hands with a tall, thin-lipped man named Rupert Hallop, who was dressed in range clothes and smelled like whiskey and horse. Hallop had a scar that ran the breadth of his forehead and a cast in one eye. He looked competent enough in an untrustworthy sort of way. He wore twin Colts on crossed belts and spoke with a vaguely Southern accent.

The second man was a greenhorn through and through. Spectacles, pink cheeks, a cotton shirt and jeans just off the sutler's shelf. He had an ornamental Smith & Wesson revolver hanging from his belt.

"This is Dr. Horace Cobb, Ruff," Colonel MacEnroe said, and Ruff shook hands with the greenhorn, too. The little man's shake was as firm as he could make it, but the hand itself was smooth, womanly, without callus or scar.

The third member of the party was a cool little fox of a man named Keep. Gregory Keep. This was his show, and after they all got through shaking hands and bowing, he sat down and told Justice what it was all about.

"Six months ago my cousin came west with five other men to go gold hunting in the Little Missouri badlands. Tom Keep was his name. He must have passed through Bismarck—maybe you met him?"

Ruff said he couldn't recall any such honor. He was watching Keep closely. The man was sharp, very sharp, with the quickness of a small animal. Under his coat flap was a Colt .32, and Ruff would have bet Keep knew well enough how to use it.

"He didn't come back?" Ruff asked after a minute.

"No. He didn't come back."

"There are a lot of men," Colonel MacEnroe put in, "who aren't coming back these days. The Sioux are unhappy again, very unhappy."

"Tom Keep was a plainsman?" Ruff asked.

"No, not really, although . . ."

Justice didn't hear the rest of it. A man had to be a fool to go into the badlands these days, and no one who didn't know the land and the ways of the Sioux was likely to come back.

"Miss Farmer's brother and her father were with Tom Keep," the colonel said.

"They didn't come back, either?"

"No, Mr. Justice, they didn't, but I'm sure they're all right. My father was very experienced."

"You intend to go looking for him?" Ruff asked.

"That's right, yes. Why shouldn't I?"

"There's a hundred reasons, Miss Farmer. Have you considered hiring someone to go have a look-see?"

"Someone like you?" she asked much too sharply—the woman was working with badly frayed nerves.

"No, miss. I've already got a job."

"I have Mr. Keep with me, Dr. Cobb, Rupert Hallop and his men. Miss Eccles and I are not afraid of a few Indians."

That was the first time in a while Ruff had heard the Sioux nation labeled "a few Indians." "There's another woman with your party?"

"Miss Gertrude Eccles. Dr. Eccles, actually," Cobb said. "She's my fiancée and assistant."

"I don't quite get your interest in this, Doctor."

"Dr. Eccles and I are interested in certain anthropological implications made by the diary."

"The diary?"

"Tom Keep kept a diary, Ruff. It was brought into Bismarck two months ago and Mr. Gregory Keep's address was found in it. It was sent to Mr. Keep's Ohio home where . . ." The colonel looked at Keep.

"Where I sat down to study it, Mr. Justice. To determine what had happened to my brother."

"That's the book there?" Ruff asked, nodding at the leather-bound volume on the colonel's desk. It appeared to be a diary; at least there was a hasp affixed to it, a broken hasp.

"Yes, that's it."

Justice picked it up, turned it over, and leaning back in his chair, opened it to the first page.

April 11, 1878

We arrive finely at Bismark and in the morning will get supplies and a fresh horse for Dougherty and be on our way again. Farmer has found us an old Arikara Indian who will take us most of the way to the badlands.

Ruff skipped ahead a way. There were many entries that held nothing but the weather—hot.

May 29, 1878

Finely showing some color as we pan. Not too good however. MacDonald bit by rattlesnake. Looks like he'll make it. We move on into badlands when he can travel. Our Arik's deserted us. Says that country's no good. Says evil things live there—Stone Warriors. We push on.

June 9

This is it! Biggest damn strike believable. Took out three hundred dollars in an hour yesterday. Bad trouble now. Samuels went down to the river and didn't come back. Body terrible beat. Terrible. Maybe because we are working too near the Indian caves up above the lone pine. Farmer says no Indian done it, no Indian he heard of, and Dougherty is crying again about them. The Stone Warriors.

No matter. We're each taking a thousand in dust and pulling out end of week.

June 14

Monday again. A thousand was too little. Might not get back soon. Hot days. A howling thing come in the night. Got two thousand in my poke. MacDonald dead from them.

That was the end of the entry and the end of the diary. Ruff frowned, closed the book, and placed it back on the colonel's desk.

"Do you know where those caves are, Ruff?" the colonel asked.

"I think so, sir. I've heard of them but not seen them. I've never had occasion to go that far into the badlands."

"No. The Sioux stay clear of the area, and it's hard, dry country. I don't think a dozen men have been in there in the last five years."

"You want me to go in, sir?" Ruff asked. "Is that it?"

"Yes, that's it. I want you to go in and take the doctor's party with you."

Ruff started to smile. His head inclined to one side

slightly. Take *them*? The little pink professor and the woman? The colonel had to be joking—but there wasn't a trace of a smile on the colonel's lips.

"It's not very wise, sir," Ruff offered.

"No." MacEnroe shook his head. "It's not, is it? I've spent the better part of the past hour trying to convince Dr. Cobb of that. He's determined to go on anyway."

"Do you understand, sir," Ruff said to the little man, "that you've entered a war zone?"

"A war zone? Everyone knows that the Sioux have drifted up to Canada. Your own military intelligence confirms that."

"No one knows what the Sioux are up to at any given time," Justice answered. "Even if the Sioux nation is drifting up to Red Cloud's Canadian camp, that doesn't mean we have no stragglers, raiders, men who want to go it on their own. There's been hard fighting out here, sir. It's left a lot of bitter feelings on both sides. And neither side shows much mercy anymore." Justice looked steadily at the professor, who only shrugged.

"It is imperative that I go in now."

"Why?"

"The Stone Warriors," the little man said.

Hallop laughed out loud and turned away quickly. Gregory Keep was fighting back a smile. Sarah Farmer wore a look of resignation, as if she were listening to a joke repeated once too often.

"What is your interest in them, sir?"

"What is my interest? I am an anthropologist, sir. A man who is devoting his life to filling in the massive gaps in our knowledge of the Indian and his life on this continent."

Colonel MacEnroe found a cigar, lit it without offering anyone else a smoke, and sat silently for a minute in his chair, veiled by a cloud of blue smoke. Then he spoke. "The professor has a charter from the Department of the Interior to explore the region and civilization of the people reported to live there."

"That is correct." The professor got a little hot under the collar himself. "What's the matter with all of you? Can't you see how remarkable this may be? A people who are not of Indian descent living in the American West."

"It's remarkable, all right," Hallop said.

"Yes," the professor turned on the guide. "I am sure that you are quite well informed on this subject, Mr. Hallop."

"How the hell well informed do you have to be to know crap when you see it."

"Please, sir," the colonel said with a nod toward the woman.

Hallop waved a disgusted hand and walked over to the window to stare out.

"This is quite important scientifically," Cobb said a little defensively. "You have no idea."

"I know it's flat impossible," Hallop shot back.

"I am sorry. You are quite wrong. It is far from impossible that the Stone Warriors exist. I know of at least two other discoveries that point to non-Indian aboriginal inhabitants of this land. That is, I speculate that they may be aboriginal. Others contend that they are the remnant of early exploration parties from northern Europe."

"In Dakota Territory!"

"The remains of giant men have been discovered in Nevada and Colorado. In California a town was terrorized by a band of red-bearded savages who spoke no known tongue, whose home was discovered to be a cave decorated with primitive devices, some Norse in their implications . . ." Cobb was hot now, but even he could see that he wasn't making much of an impression on Hallop.

Nor on Keep, for that matter. These two were interested not in legends but in finding the body and belongings of the missing men. Chiefly, Ruff thought, in finding the belongings. A thousand dollars a week in gold dust.

Justice was thoughtful. He had no wish to go into the badlands. The professor had a scientific motive; the men wanted to find that gold, badly. Miss Farmer perhaps just wished to see her brother and father buried properly—although she seemed to be clinging to the hope that they had somehow survived out there.

Ruff doubted they had, doubted it seriously, and he felt sorry for the woman.

"So then, Colonel MacEnroe," Cobb went on briskly, "we shall leave in the morning."

"Mr. Justice hasn't given you his answer yet," MacEnroe said.

"Justice—he is employed by the army, is he not?"

"He is. However, I am not ordering him to take this assignment. It may be that he will choose not to lead you into the badlands. Ruff?"

"What?" Justice's mind had been elsewhere. "We have a party of cavalry going with us, sir?"

"Six men. I really can't spare them, but . . ."

"Mr. Hallop has three armed men with him," Miss Farmer said.

And that, Justice thought, was interesting. Very interesting. Just who was in charge of this group? Gregory Keep, who had hired Hallop, or Hallop, who had hired the guns? It was a bad mixture—science and gold, a young woman, badlands savages.

"Mr. Justice still hasn't answered us," Sarah Farmer said.

Ruff lifted his cold blue eyes. He looked at Sarah, deliberately taking in the curves and lines of her body until she blushed and was forced to look away, her ears crimson.

"Sure," Ruff said, "I'll be happy to take you in—if I can't talk you out of going altogether."

"Of course not. Don't be absurd," Dr. Horace Cobb responded.

"Maybe Justice believes in ghosts and bogies," Hallop said. "Maybe he's scared of the Stone Warriors, too."

"Maybe so," Ruff answered quietly. "Maybe so."

But Hallop couldn't understand that. He was the type of man who lived in a small world bounded on one side by greed, on the other by violence. He accepted nothing he hadn't seen with his own eyes, and misinterpreted half of what he had seen.

Just now Hallop was making two errors. He was discounting the Stone Warriors out of hand and misinterpreting the caution in Ruff Justice. Those errors would cost Rupert Hallop, cost him dearly.

When the others were gone, Colonel MacEnroe dipped into his bottom desk drawer for the bottle of bourbon he kept there. He smiled, sighed, and leaned back in his chair.

"Sorry about this one, Ruff, but I didn't know what else to do. The Interior Department leaned on the War Department, which leaned on Regiment, and there you are."

"Can't be helped." Ruff shrugged. "There isn't anyone else to go to out here but the army, is there?"

"No, no, there isn't." MacEnroe finished his drink. "I hate to lay it off on you, though."

"It may be very interesting."

"It may be damned interesting if you hit Sioux trouble, yes. You think those gun-toting cowboys of Hallop's know anything about Indian fighting?"

"I'll have your men, sir. By the way, do I get any choice there? I'd sure like to have Ray Hardistein or any other experienced NCO."

"Can't handle the men, Ruff?" The colonel smiled.

"I'm not much good at it. I'd like someone along I know and have worked with."

"Hardistein's gone south with Lieutenant Short to chase those Cheyenne reservation-jumpers, so he's out. Really I can't spare anyone, Ruff, let alone a first rate NCO. You understand that, don't you?"

"Yes, sir." Ruff understood it. The colonel was being cooperative. On paper. There would be no repercussions about his handling of Dr. Cobb's party. But he wasn't going to strip himself of fighting men either just so some half-baked academic could ride into the badlands looking for red-bearded cavemen.

"I'm sorry you have to be involved in this at all, actually. God knows I've got other assignments I could use you on. This must strike you as rather amusing, Ruffin."

"No, sir, I can't say that."

"You can't mean you think there's anything to this?"

"No? Maybe not." Justice shrugged, but said nothing more. Still he was remembering. Remembering the winter he had found the Sioux—the Sioux with his eyes plucked out, his flesh burned to charred leather, and every single bone in his body from fingertip to skull broken at least once. Or the time he had found the elk with its head stripped of flesh and hide—only the head. The animal had been gutted and something had been at the haunches, devouring it raw. Something that had not been wolf or grizzly, lynx or coyote.

"We'll have our look-see," Justice said. He rose, putting on his white hat, picking up his sheathed rifle. "No guarantees on this one, sir. I wish to hell— Well, I suppose you've tried to talk the women into not going out there."

"You've spoken to Miss Farmer," Colonel MacEnroe said with a helpless gesture. "You've seen how she is. Miss Eccles is no better—another scientist." The colonel almost shuddered at the word. He rose and walked around from behind his desk to escort Ruff to the door. "I'm making light of this, Ruff—maybe because I'm worried. I don't like this little party's makeup. I don't like the smell of Hallop and Keep. They stink of greed, Ruff, plain greed. The women have no business being here at all. And the professor—I'm not sure he's all there. He's dreaming of glory and discovery, but he hasn't got the sense to see the very real possibilities for bloodshed. It's a hell of a crew to saddle you with."

Justice had been thinking much the same thing. There were ominous overtones to this little expedition, the feeling that things just weren't quite right, that beyond the reckless folly lay a real and conscious menace.

It didn't help any to step outside a minute later and come face to face with the man who wanted him dead.

... ... ... have been ...

# 4

Regis Cavanaugh was a killer. He would go on killing
until someone stopped him with a bullet or a noose.
Brought up in postwar Alabama, he had a grudge
against the world, especially against anything that
smelled of the North and, in particular, against Northern soldiers. There couldn't have been many places in
the world Regis Cavanaugh would have disliked more
than Fort Lincoln. But his dark little eyes lighted
with savage glee when Ruff Justice stepped out of the
orderly room into the cold light of the Dakota afternoon.

Regis Cavanaugh was slouched against the wheel of
a spring buggy. He wore a black leather vest over a
black silk shirt and had a red scarf knotted around his
neck. He hadn't changed. He looked older than his
twenty-four years, but then Regis Cavanaugh had been
born old. There were still warrants out on him in the
South, where Cavanaugh had taken to sniping at occu-
pying soldiers when he was but twelve years old.
Cavanaugh hadn't stopped shooting at people yet, although he was legal in Dakota as far as Justice knew.

"Hello, Cavanaugh."

"Mr. Justice," Cavanaugh said with a little snicker.

"Haven't seen you for a while."

"Not since Fort Worth."

"No. That soldier ever recover? A shot in the back can be awful bad."

"Damn you—he was drawing!"

"Sure."

Cavanaugh had a thing about his courage; whether he suspected it himself Ruff didn't know. He knew that Cavanaugh couldn't stand to be taunted about it. Maybe it was because he had had four older brothers who had gone off to war, served honorably, and been killed while he sat at home holding his mother's apron string. Maybe it was just that Regis Cavanaugh was a little mad.

"Is there some trouble here?" Professor Cobb found the two men braced and ready, and he glanced from one to the other, trying to understand. In Cobb's world things didn't come to violence.

"I want this man off the crew," Justice said.

"Off?" Cobb blinked his eyes rapidly. "I don't understand. He's just been hired—we can't just fire him."

"Off. Who hired him, by the way?" Ruff was talking to Cobb, but his eyes were fixed on Cavanaugh, watching the gunman's hands. No sane man would try to get away with murder on an army post, but Cavanaugh wasn't quite sane, and Justice knew it.

"Mr. Hallop hired Cavanaugh and his friends." Cobb looked distressed and confused. "What *is* this anyway? Must we have petty arguments?"

"It's so damned petty," Ruff Justice said, "that if he's not out of my sight in thirty seconds, I'm going to kill him. You've hired yourself something besides a gun, Professor. You've hired a piece of slime, a scab that walks around pretending it's a man."

Cavanaugh started to do it then. His lip curled back and he twitched, his hand moving toward his gun, but he just didn't have what it took to try Ruff Justice face to face.

"I hate to see things begin this way," Cobb said. "I'm sure that whatever it is, we can resolve it."

"That's right," Justice replied. "We can resolve it. Why didn't I think of that? Just have Cavanaugh here bring the dead back to life."

"I don't . . ." Cobb was flustered. "I don't know what you're referring to, of course, but we can't promise a man employment and then fire him because one of the other men doesn't care for him."

"You'll fire this one. He's a back-shooting murderer and I'll not step outside this fort with him around—unless it's to settle things." Ruff moved in yet another step, towering over Cavanaugh, who hadn't changed his slouched position. "No, I guess he wouldn't want to step outside with me. Get rid of him, Cobb, or consider me gone."

"I don't . . . I'll have to speak to Mr. Hallop and Mr. Keep. I just can't understand this sort of behavior."

"You can start packing, Regis, unless you want to take me up on the invitation."

"No one's told me to move along but you," Cavanaugh said. He was starting to raise his hackles some, to puff up a little, and it made Ruff suspicious enough to glance around. Two men he didn't know were in back of him, slowly easing down the plankwalk in front of the orderly room.

"Mack!" Justice called out, not loudly, but clearly. After a minute Fort Lincoln's massive first sergeant appeared in the doorway.

"What is it, Mr. Justice?"

"If you'll look to your left, Mack, there's a couple of gentlemen who have an idea of causing some mischief. Keep an eye on them, will you?"

"Sure thing, Ruffin."

"Now then, Cavanaugh, which way are you going to

have it? I won't turn my back on you, it'll have to be faceup."

"Damn you, Justice," Cavanaugh sputtered.

"How is it going to be?" Ruff repeated.

Again, for a single moment, Ruff thought that Cavanaugh's pride might be strong enough to prod him into it, but he wasn't quite ready to die, pride or no. He spun around and stalked off toward a hitched gray horse, Cobb's eyes following him helplessly. The two backup men trailed after Regis Cavanaugh, and when all three were mounted, they turned and rode very slowly out of Fort Lincoln.

"That about it, is it?" Mack Pierce asked with a chuckle. The first sergeant held a shotgun in his hands. His red face was cheerful but a little disappointed. Mack wouldn't have minded a first-rate scrap. He was overweight and lethargic these days and he didn't like traveling much, but if the fighting would come to his door, why, that was just fine.

"Looks like that's all, Mack. Thanks."

"Did I hear you say that man's name was Cavanaugh?" Pierce asked.

"Yes. That was the name, Regis Cavanaugh."

"Damn! I wish he had started something. I've heard that name before. He is the one . . . ?"

"He's the one, Mack."

"Well, damn my eyes," the big sergeant said, "I wish he *had* started something." Pierce turned and went in, still muttering.

"Well," Professor Cobb said, "now you've done it, haven't you, Mr. Justice?"

"Yes, I think so."

"Don't congratulate yourself. Those men were a part of our expedition."

"The dirty part. They were killers, Professor. There's paper out on them in a dozen states."

"But not here! I knew about Cavanaugh's background —Hallop explained that he wanted to go straight."

"Straight to that lost gold." Ruffin T. Justice looked more closly at the reforming professor. "How far east are you from anyway? You must live a long way from anything wild or dangerous, Cobb, you know that? You must never have walked the same street or ridden the same trail as these bastards and those like them. I can hardly believe there's men as ignorant as you. The man's a killer."

"Mr. Justice would want to execute him, I'm sure," a strange voice said. As Ruff turned, she continued, "That was what you were trying to do just now, wasn't it, Mr. Justice? Although the law in Dakota Territory has nothing at all against Regis Cavanaugh—I know, I checked."

"Uh, Dr. Gertrude Eccles," Cobb said awkwardly. It was a hell of a time to attempt an introduction.

Dr. Gertrude Eccles came forward. She wore a man's brown cotton shirt, a man's twill trousers. She had her light-brown hair pinned up severely. Her gray eyes were magnified by the bifocals she wore.

"That Cavanaugh isn't wanted in Dakota is a breakdown in the system, ma'am. It shows the law doesn't always do what it's meant to. He ought to be wanted every place on this planet. There ought to be a big fat reward for the man who would walk up and shoot him in his malignant little brain."

"Oh, glory!" Dr. Gertrude Eccles said, mockingly lifting her hands to the sky. "The Western hero come to save us from the evil of mankind. With steel and hot lead—I once read a dime novel, Mr. Justice; it is always 'hot lead,' isn't it?"

"Could be, I wouldn't know."

Hallop was running toward them. His face was flushed with anger. He stopped, chest heaving, to look from Ruff to Cobb, to the main gate of Lincoln.

"I heard that Cavanaugh's gone, that you ran him off."

"You heard right," Ruff said. He took off his hat and wiped back his long dark hair, winking at Gertrude Eccles, who went stiff with indignation.

"Why! For God's sake, I know Cavanaugh wasn't much, but we need fighting men along, don't we?"

"You don't need a killer like Cavanaugh."

"Maybe not." Hallop shrugged. His scarred face didn't look quite so fierce now. He rested his hands negligently on his twin Colts and looked skyward. "Hell, I don't know what to do. Keep hired me to run things—horses, campsites, grub, security. Have you any idea how hard it is to come by men out here just now? Men who will go out onto the plains."

"We'll have a look around Bismarck. Maybe we can find someone," Ruff said.

"Yes," Gertrude Eccles said, clapping her hands together, "some of *Justice*'s friends." She shook her head heavily and said to Cobb, "Horace, this is really too much. We should have kept to our original intention of bringing a strictly scientific entourage. It was a mistake to allow that Farmer woman, Mr. Keep, and"—her eyes went to Ruff Justice as she searched for a suitable term—"others into this."

"The Secretary of the Interior wouldn't allow any sort of expedition without army support, dear." Cobb mouthed the last word very softly and looked away quickly as he said it. Justice grinned and Gertrude flushed with anger and embarrassment.

She was going to say something, but Tom Keep and Sarah Farmer arrived just then. Explanations were passed around again and Keep said philosophically, "Well, then we need some new men."

"We'll have the soldiers," Sarah noted.

"Yes, but they won't want to build our fires, saddle

our horses, any of a dozen things. And if we decide to stay on in the badlands, we'll need a work crew."

"Mr. Justice has indicated that he knows where all of the good men are to be located," Gertrude Eccles said with a sniff.

"I think we can probably dig up a few hands," Ruff told Keep, "if you're sure you need some more people."

"Yes, we will. We might want some men to stay on with us. I don't know how this is going to go. It depends, well . . ."

"On whether or not you find your brother's gold."

"Yes," Keep said, shrugging, "something like that." He grinned boyishly and Ruff smiled in return. It was funny, but of all the men he had the idea that Keep could be the most dangerous. There was something furtive and cunning about Gregory Keep. Or maybe that was all illusion; perhaps, as Gertrude Eccles has suggested, after a time you didn't trust anyone very much.

"Mr. Justice?"

Ruff turned to find Corporal Alvin Duggs behind him. Duggs and Justice had spent some time together once in a buffalo wallow with half a hundred Cheyenne riding in a circle around them. Ruff liked the blond kid who wore the brim of his hat folded up and his sun-faded uniform shirt with the cuffs rolled back.

"Are you going along with us, Duggs?"

"I reckon, Mr. Justice. I was told to report to you. I've got six men assigned to me. Whatever you're up to, I guess we're a part of it."

"Fine." He glanced at Keep. "What we'll do, I think, is ride into Bismarck and see if we can find some civilian help for these people." Keep nodded agreement and Ruff went on. "If you'll get your men outfitted, Alvin, and then meet us in town—say, two hours?"

"That's time enough," the kid agreed.

"All right. That's all there is to it. Bring yourselves enough ammunition, will you, Corporal?"

"Going west, are we, Mr. Justice?"

"Yes, that's right. We're going west."

"Do you mind telling us what for? I'm kind of curious— the men will want to know."

"No, not at all," Justice said. "There's gold out there, Corporal. Gold, and possibly a band of red-bearded giants who can't be killed. The professor would like to have a look at them and measure their skulls."

"Sure," Alvin Duggs said with a laugh. "Mr. Justice, you're a prize, you truly are. I'll tell the men it's a perimeter patrol and escort." Satisfied, Duggs walked off, chuckling to himself.

Ruff walked back to his quarters adjacent to the enlisted barracks, stripped down, washed, and shaved. Then for a time he sat naked on his bunk, staring at the wall.

From time to time he had assignments he didn't care for, some that seemed plain foolish or dangerous. This seemed both, and already Ruff disliked it intensely.

They had tried to bully him off the job before they had even gotten out the gate. Every single one in this party was either a greenhorn or a grifter, some perhaps both. Hallop was nothing but a gunny—what in hell did they need gunhands along for? Keep was looking for gold, nothing else, that was obvious to Justice at the start. As for the professor and his mannish assistant, they were just plain crazy. As was the government for backing this particular expedition at this time in that part of the country.

As was Ruff Justice for accepting this assignment instead of laughing, turning on his heel, and getting the hell out of sight.

A knock on the door interrupted these morose thoughts. "Yeah?"

"Justice, it's me, Alvin Duggs."

"Come on in, Corporal."

"I've got the patrol all lined out," Duggs said after he had come into the room. He stood against the wall, arms folded on his chest, boyish and confident at once. Duggs had had two years at Lincoln already, before that three years of war and soldiering down south. He was young, but he knew his way around on the trail and behind the sights of a Springfield rifle.

He asked Ruff, "Did you want us to go on ahead with the wagons, or wait for you, Mr. Justice?"

"They're ready to roll out already?"

"Some big hurry-up." Duggs shrugged. "They said they had to get into Bismarck and hire some help. Help for what?"

"Probably some men to protect the ladies from the troopers." Ruff cracked.

"Sir, I hate to say it, but they don't need a lot of protecting, although that Miss Farmer has the proper looks. She's hard, ain't she? That's my impression."

"Not half as hard as the other one," Justice answered. And maybe she's just scared, or defensive. That was the way he measured up Sarah Farmer. How had she gotten tied up with Keep anyway? He'd have to ask.

"Go on ahead, then, or stay put?" Duggs asked.

Ruff shook his head. "Go on into Bismarck if they can't wait for me to put my pants on," Justice answered. "Just don't let them take off onto the plains before we're all together and get things understood."

"Things?"

"Things like the fact that I'm in charge here, Corporal Duggs, for better or for worse, and as much as they might want to go out there and get themselves scalped, I'm not going to let it happen."

"I see ..." Duggs hesitated. "This other business, Ruff, this stuff about the Stone Warriors—it's a joke, ain't it? I been asking around and I ran up against someone who told me it's gospel, but that was George

Lewison, and you can't believe half of what he says. I mean"—Duggs looked embarrassed for asking—"there ain't a thing behind it, is there?"

Justice wasn't smiling when he answered, "I don't know, Duggs. I've heard stories, seen a thing or two that needed some better explanation than what I got. Let's put it this way: there's men living in the badlands, men who don't like outsiders coming in. Maybe they're Indian, maybe they're not; all we know at this point is they like to take a man and crush him slowly to death, to break every bone in his body, every single bone, literally. Just lay it out to your men if there's any that don't understand. They kill, Duggs, and they like it. Whatever else, whoever else the Stone Warriors are, they are killers."

Duggs left, not very satisfied with the answer Ruff had given him. It wasn't much of an answer, really, but Justice didn't know any more than the professor did. He had heard the tales, though, and if you couldn't believe half of them, still you were struck with the constant theme of blood lust that ran through them. *If* the Stone Warriors existed, they were savage beyond belief, savage enough to frighten hell out of hardened Sioux warriors.

Ruff rose and started to dress, tugging his trousers on first.

Pocono had been the first man Ruff had heard talk about the Stone Warriors. Old Poke, who knew this country upside down and backward and wasn't known for exaggerating. Old Poke, who had ended things with the biggest lie of all . . . but poke had always told things straight to Ruff before that last ride, and Justice believed him.

According to Poke, there were caves out there above the Little Missouri, where it carves its tortuous way through the badlands. Caves with strange paintings on the walls, ships of a long-ago time, a faraway place, like none Pocono had ever seen—they certainly weren't Indian canoes.

There were supposed to be piles of ashes in the caves, ashes mingled with broken bones. The ashes of dead men killed by the Stone Warriors.

The Sioux had their own theory, their own legend.

Long ago, before the first man, the first Indian, had been made by Manitou, savage giants roamed the land to the west of the pipestone quarry, the great red rock. They were a savage race given to eating their young. All of their weak were killed at birth, since there could be no Stone Warrior who was not strong and powerful.

They had come from over the moon, said the Sioux, in the time of ice, the time of endless winter. Some said they had sailed across the sky, others that Manitou had banished them from his heavens. But they had come.

Then the Indian, the Sioux, and the Cheyenne had come, sprung from Manitou's loins. Men upon the earth, and they had driven the Stone Warriors back, although the price of war had been heavy.

Finally the leaders of the Sioux and Cheyenne had counciled, chiefly two war leaders named Bear and Wolf.

"Now we must kill them all," Wolf, the Cheyenne, had insisted, "now that we have driven them to the end of the earth."

The Sioux, Bear, had disagreed. "No people must vanish entirely from this world. Manitou has let them be for a reason. It is not up to us to kill them, every last one. We suffer snakes to live, coyotes, scorpions. A few so that the world remembers them."

"These are not men," Wolf had objected.

"They are creatures of Manitou. Not men, not like us, but they exist. Therefore, leave them to this terrible land"—he meant the bandlands, twisted, dry, violent, and cursed—"and let a handful live."

"Only a few. I will not suffer them to grow strong again. I will let twelve live and ask Manitou that they not increase. Only twelve. Twelve who will live in this terrible land. Never again shall any Cheyenne go into this land, never again shall any Stone Warrior come onto the plains. That must be how it is, that is how it shall be."

That was all the Indians knew about the Stone Warriors—this legend that had been passed down to explain the inexplicable. Red-bearded savages living in the badlands. That was all the Indians knew, and all any man knew. Ruff supposed a scientist like Cobb would be intrigued by the possibilities, would need to know.

He only hoped that Cobb had been listening when they spoke of violence, of blood and piles of human ash.

Justice rode his big black horse into Bismarck. The skies were gray and limitless, the grass long and green. The wind was cold, lifting the fringes of Justice's buckskins as he rode.

Across the saddlebows he carried his buckskin-sheathed .56 Spencer repeater; behind him, his bed-roll with India rubber groundsheet, his slicker, and his buffalo coat; more canned goods than he normally would carry; a hundred round box of .56-caliber ammunition, and another of .44s; a ledger book, a spare knife, and a volume of Shakespeare.

Bismarck seemed to be busy. There was traffic on the river. In the last year or so a few shallow draft riverboats had dared to come upstream. The Indians had a hell of a good time attacking the paddle wheelers, but since the pilots were smart enough to stay in the middle of the river, not much damage had been done to date.

There was a thin rooster tail of dust rising to the south of Bismarck, and Ruff smiled as he made it out. It, and the multicolored wagons that were raising the dust. The gypsies were pulling out—and be damned to them, their king, Jocko, and all.

"Excepting Rachel," Ruff said to the horse, which twitched an ear and snorted once, understanding nothing but liking the sound of its new master's voice. Ruff laughed, patted the strapping black's neck, and lifted it into a canter.

Ahead lay Bismarck—sullen, silent, dark against the plains—and beyond that the glittering river. And beyond the river the land of the Sioux and the Cheyenne, and beyond that the end of the world—the land of the Stone Warriors.

# 5

He found the Cobb party at the Butter & Eggs Restaurant. It had always been one of Ruff's own favorite places to eat—of course, there weren't but three or four to choose from. But Molly McCormick, who ran the place, believed in putting as much food on a platter as she could, in making it as good as she could, and in charging as little as possible. She was a rare woman, was Molly McCormick.

The woman was a bulky, cheerful blonde. She liked men in that rare way given only to a few women. She simply liked their company, liked feeding them, bandaging them, tending them. Her own husband had died crossing the prairie in '66. Jack McCormick must have been a hell of a man in his own right; Molly had never remarried and her eyes still got misty when she spoke of "Big Jack."

Cobb was in the corner with the two women, sipping at coffee. They had a map spread out on the table before them. Justice recognized the map immediately—the Donaldson map, not worth the paper it was on.

Donaldson had been a lieutenant under Crook, and by all accounts a fairly competent line officer. He had been wounded at Battle Fork and, after mustering out, had looked around for a way to make a living. He had written some rather lurid and quite spurious memoirs, which had him as their hero, rescuing Indian princesses, fighting grizzly bears with his empty hands, besting Sitting Bull in a bow-and-arrow contest—all the dime-novel gear. It had been accepted in the East, and Donaldson had made himself a good dollar from his work.

A map drawn by Donaldson had appeared at the same time. That map had gotten dozens of people killed, hundreds lost, and more broken. It had no relationship to reality, once the Missouri was crossed. A pass to Oregon, which had never existed, was plainly shown through the Rockies. The Black Hills adjoined the Moreau River instead of lying south of the Belle Fourche. Either Donaldson himself hadn't drawn up the map or he had been criminally negligent.

"Good morning again, Mr. Justice," Professor Cobb said coolly. "I've been laying out a trail for us to follow, if you'll just give it your final approval."

Ruff glanced at the map, at the line Cobb had sketched on it. "You'd only miss the badlands by a couple hundred miles if you follow that, Cobb."

"What do you mean? I *have* been in the field before, you know, in Africa—"

"Maybe you had better maps in Africa. This one is just no good." Justice took a chair, reversed it, and sat down, pouring himself a cup of coffee. The act seemed to offend Cobb, Gertrude Eccles, and Sarah Farmer.

"It's the best map available for this region," Cobb said defensively.

"I don't doubt that. It's no good, Cobb. Believe me." He sipped at his coffee and smiled at Sarah Farmer, who actually flinched.

"You, I suppose, know the way," Gertrude Eccles said, her voice rising at the end of the sentence.

"Yes, I do. Have we hired on any camp hands yet."

"Mr. Keep and Mr. Hallop are out doing that now."

"I'd like to catch up with them. Any idea where they were going to start?"

"The saloons, one supposes," Cobb said. He was still gazing at his map wistfully. He had drawn such a nice line on it, too.

"Right. I'll catch up later then." Ruff stood. "Thanks for the coffee."

Outside, it was cool, the wind blowing leaves and litter up the street. A freight wagon was loading up in front of the general store, probably rolling out to Sanderson's Julep mine to the east of town. Ruff stepped into the stirrup, swung aboard, and walked the big black toward the nearest saloon, the Down and Dirty.

He didn't see Keep's horse there, nor Hallop's. He did recognize the gray tied at the rail, however. Regis Cavanaugh must be getting good and tanked up. With what ideas whirling through his little head? Revenge? Cavanaugh was a known sniper-killer. He liked to shoot from ambush—there was much less chance of getting himself hurt that way. He liked to kill soldiers and anything or anyone attached to the army—at least he had in the past.

The smartest thing to do at that juncture might have been to walk in to the Down and Dirty, deliberately pick a fight with Regis Cavanaugh, and have done with the man.

It wasn't Justice's way. He intended, however, to keep a sharp eye on the back trail. Regis Cavanaugh carrying a mad was all they needed on top of the Sioux and the Stone Warriors, the inexperience, and the weather.

Ruff looked skyward. It was clouding up a little to the north. Not much, a few low bulwarks of gray against the sky, but Ruff didn't like the electric-blue color of the sky near the horizon. Nor did he like the smell of it, the feel of it. It was very early for snow, but he had seen it blow out of Canada before this when it should have been too early.

Frowning, he rode on toward the Bucket of Blood, Art Townsend's place, and swung down. Keep was inside with Hallop and Alvin Duggs. The three men stood at the bar talking to two down-and-out-looking men, possibly a part of that big sheep operation that had folded when the grass fire burned out the J & T down south. That had left half a hundred men, many of them Basques, stranded.

Duggs was having himself a morning beer and he glanced sheepishly at Ruff, finishing it quickly. Ruff grinned.

"Any luck?" Justice asked the corporal. Keep turned those dark little eyes his way. He also smiled, but there wasn't a lot of humor in Gregory Keep's smile.

Gregory Keep? Was he? Who said that this was the dead man's brother? The idea flitted through Ruff's mind and then was tucked away for future reference.

"We've got six people, that should be enough."

"Sheepmen?"

"Yes, all but one."

"Bronk Hodges, you know him," Alvin Duggs said.

"Yes, I know him," Ruff said. What was left of him. Bronk was going down hard and fast, riding the bottle to oblivion. "If he's drinking, there's no sense in hiring him on."

"He's not drinking, Ruff."

"He says?"

Keep interrupted, "Look, Justice, it would be nice to have a dozen strong men, range-tough, plains-wise, faithful and brave, but dammit, we have to take what we can get. You've already given the boot to Cavanaugh and his men. We can't spend the rest of the year trying to hire people that'll suit you. That's the way it's got to be."

As much as Justice hated to admit it, Keep was right. It wouldn't be easy to find half a dozen men who needed work badly enough to go out onto the plains knowing the Sioux were out there.

"All right," Ruff said with a shrug. "You men been warned?" he asked the sheepherders.

"Yes, sir."

"All right. Keep, let's have at it. Alvin, shake the dust off, finish that beer and let's get rolling."

It wasn't all that quick. The new hands had to be outfitted. Not a one of them had a rain slicker; one of them didn't even have a horse, which was the reason he had signed on: Keep had promised him one.

Then there were sacks of beans, flour, rice, sides of bacon, cases of tinned beef, to be loaded. Keep wasn't planning on running fast if it came to that, but then no one in the party seemed to think that such an event might come to pass. It was a picnic, a scientific expedition complete with little campfires at night, the wide open spaces, and starry nights.

They didn't want to hear about the Sioux or Regis Cavanaugh, the wolves or the hard weather.

Justice watched as they loaded the two wagons. He squatted in the shade of the general store's awning, his face expressionless. The troopers, he noticed, seemed as green as everyone else, with the exception of Duggs. Colonel MacEnroe hadn't exactly sent his first-line squad.

Duggs himself seemed to take this as a break from his regular duties, a happy little excursion with women to look at and everything.

"Looks like we're ready," Gregory Keep said. He stood over Ruff looking down, a slight smile on his lips. "Want to lead out?"

"No. You go ahead, Keep. Take the road west as long as it lasts. By then it'll be suppertime, or near to it. Get 'em rolling, that's all."

"And you?"

"I want to say good-bye to a few friends," Ruff Justice said, and his eyes, Keep noticed, were on the Down and Dirty Saloon across the dusty street.

"All right. We'll be expecting you at night camp. Take it easy, won't you?" The smile was deeper now, more cynical.

"I'll be there," Justice told him. "Just hold them west."

Keep strolled off, pausing to light a cigar. He managed to cast a last backward glance at Justice as he did so.

"What do you want me to do, Ruff?" Corporal Duggs asked.

"Just what you're supposed to, Alvin. Ride escort, watch your flanks, and keep an eye behind you."

"Regis Cavanaugh, you mean."

"That's right."

"You're not going to tangle with him, are you, Mr. Justice?"

"Not unless I can't help it. Get on now. And stay alert."

Duggs promised that he would. Justice stood in the narrow strip of shadow cast by the awning in front of the general store and watched the expedition form up.

Hallop was sitting his roan, watching the sheepherders silently. He had his hat tugged low, darkening his face. It was difficult to make out his expression, but Ruff would have bet he was more than a little unhappy. He would have far preferred to have Regis Cavanaugh at his side.

Or had Cavanaugh been Keep's idea? You couldn't tell what Keep was thinking. Ruff couldn't decide now, as he watched the small man ride up in front of the general store, swing down, and strut up to the first wagon, where Sarah Farmer was being helped up by the storekeeper.

Sarah Farmer was a hell of a fine-looking woman—a little stiff, a little nervous, but there was stuff in her. Ruff still wanted to know how she had come to be tangled up with Keep, but maybe the answer to that was simple. Maybe he had known where his brother's prospecting partner had lived and had written to inform her of his intentions. But knowing Keep, the opposite seemed more likely—that he would wish to prevent Sarah or anyone else from knowing that there was any gold in the badlands.

Cobb and the woman rode in the second wagon. Gertrude Eccles: you couldn't make a lot out of her. Just a cardboard woman in spectacles. She seemed devoted to Cobb, but then, who knew what was going on in her head.

It was fifteen minutes before Keep signaled the rest of the party and led out. Him first, with Hallop not far behind. Then came two soldiers followed by Sarah Farmer's wagon, which was presently being driven by Alvin Duggs, his horse hitched on behind. Then, two more cavalry soldiers and the supply wagon, followed by the bulk of the party, the hired laborers and remaining soldiers.

Justice watched until they were all out of sight, until the dust had settled and Bismarck's main street was empty. He watched the clouds build to the north, watched the kid rolling a hoop down the plankwalk, followed by a yapping yellow hound. He watched two women discuss a bonnet in the store window for most of an hour, watched a dragonfly hum past on its way to the gleaming river.

Then he watched as the saloon doors opened and Regis Cavanaugh, followed by his two drunken sidekicks, emerged. They mounted without looking up or down the street and trailed out westward. Ruff gave them five minutes, then mounted himself, heeling the big black. In another minute he was riding through

the willows west of town, through the marsh grass
and cattails rife with mosquitoes and deerfly, cutting
toward the high ground south of the trail.

He beat them there easily. Swinging down, Ruff
bellied to the rim of the knoll, his Spencer in hand.
The three men were still distant stick figures beneath
a cloud-spattered sky, their horses moving at a walk.

Justice whistled softly as he levered a round into
the breech of his .56 Spencer repeater.

An ant crawled across his hand and he watched it
for a moment before blowing it off with a puff of
breath. Behind him the black stamped impatient feet.

Cavanaugh was within two hundred yards now and
Justice was looking down the barrel of that Spencer at
him. It was a vast temptation, but Justice lowered his
sights and touched off, sending a round into the earth
in front of Cavanaugh's big gray horse.

The horse reared up and tossed its head in panic.
Cavanaugh was grabbing for his holstered Remington
and trying to keep the startled animal under control
at the same time. One of his soldiers started spraying
the hills with pistol fire, to Ruff's delight. Maybe the
man thought the Sioux were coming down on them.

But Cavanaugh knew. He was no fool; as much as
Ruff disliked him, he had to admit that. He knew the
sound of the big buffalo gun, knew that only a handful
of men carried Spencers anymore. He knew, all right.

Cavanaugh sat his horse looking toward the low
knoll. Then, ever so slowly he turned his horse and
headed back toward Bismarck, his two cronies beside
him.

Now Cavanaugh knew. He knew that Justice was
onto him, that more than one man could snipe at his
enemies. He knew one other thing if he knew Ruff
Justice at all: the next shot would be more than a
warning.

Justice got to his feet and stood watching the depart-

ing outlaws. It might have been a mistake—a mistake
to let them live at all.

He shook his head, damning the sense of honor he
carried with him, the notion that a man doesn't kill
blindly, from ambush, out of hatred, that one who
does is no man at all. One thing he knew: Cavanaugh
had no such sense of honor. If he had the chance, he
would kill.

Ruff swung aboard the big black, sheathing his rifle
as he mounted. Then with the slightest pressure of his
knees, he moved the horse out, following in the wake
of the wagon train, onto the plains where the Sioux
and the Cheyenne roamed, where any white was an
interloper, an enemy ... where the Stone Warriors
lurked.

# 6

Ruff Justice found the camp at dusk. They had two small fires going, fires that Ruff would have extinguished before sundown if it had been up to him. He'd hoped that Alvin Duggs would have had the sense to do it. They weren't going to hide from the Sioux on the open plains, but there was no need to flaunt their presence—and by the size and number of their fires announce what size party they were.

There were sentries out, at least. Spread far and thin. After dark they wouldn't be able to see an infiltrating buffalo herd.

Justice had no taste for this, though on other occasions he had brought greenhorns onto the plains. Maybe it was the vast flat emptiness that lulled them, but they seemed unable to accept the danger that lived out here. And as a result, some of those Justice had brought out had never made it back.

Maybe he could show Sarah Farmer and Professor Cobb the graves.

He swung down near the supply wagon, slipped the bit, unsaddled, and walked to the nearest fire, where

Alvin Duggs sat with two of his soldiers, two of the former sheepherders.

"Wonderin' when you'd be rolling in, Mr. Justice."

"We don't really need fires, Duggs. You know better than that."

"You'd have to speak to the professor about that. He wants them lit."

"We're in charge of security here, Alvin."

"Yes, we are, and a hell of a lot of good it does to be in charge when no one will take your orders."

Duggs was right there, and he was angry about it. He'd also been drinking, Ruff noticed. His breath was a fine whiskey-scented mist. Next to the corporal, who had his shirt unbuttoned at the top, his cuffs rolled back, was Bronk Hodges.

Bronk used to be a teamster, and a good one, but the bottle had gotten to him. He didn't have any work in Bismarck, hadn't the guts to leave, and so he hung on. The firelight was reddening his slack, beefy face. He eyed Justice with drunken belligerence.

"How you doing, Bronk?"

"Me? All right, I guess, Ruffin T. Justice. Been a time since I was in a saddle all day, but I'm making it."

"Good. Happy with the job? The pay and all."

"Sure." Bronk's eyes narrowed.

"Glad to hear it." Justice got to his feet and started kicking dirt onto the fire to kill it. "Oh, Bronk, by the way—there's not going to be any drinking on this trail. All right?" he said mildly.

"No. Whatever you say, Ruffin T. Justice," the big man answered.

"Fine. Toss it out, then."

"What are you talkin' about?" The fire was out but for a few last softly glowing embers. Across these Ruff Justice faced the old teamster.

"I'm talking about whiskey, Bronk, remember? I

won't have you drinking on this trek; I won't have you giving it to the soldiers. Dump it out on the ground."

"Like hell I will," Bronk exploded.

"You will," Justice replied. "You will or you'll start for Bismarck, leaving that company horse behind."

"You'd make a man walk that far, with the Sioux around close?"

"That's right, Bronk."

"And who made you company boss?"

"I elected myself. I'm boss until someone fires me."

"Maybe I can do it." Bronk got to his feet. He was as tall as Ruff, but thirty to forty pounds heavier. There was a silence around the fire, men backing away from potential trouble.

"You can't, Bronk," Justice said with quiet conviction. "You know that—you just can't take me anymore. Toss the whiskey and let's all get some sleep."

"Dammit, Ruff!" Bronk's hands waved around helplessly. "I can't make it without whiskey, and you know it."

"Then you should have stuck close to a saloon, Bronk. It's not personal, you know that, but I can't have my people liquored up. The Sioux would have your throats cut while you slept—you'd never even open an eye."

"Ruff . . . !" Bronk's eyes were pleading.

"Give it to me." Justice stuck out a hand, and after a moment's decision the green bottle was passed to Ruff Justice, who uncorked it and poured the whiskey onto the last of the embers, extinguishing them. He tossed the bottle into the ashes.

"Can I talk to you, Alvin?"

"Sure, Ruff," the corporal said. He was a little shamefaced. He should have been, and Ruff let him know it after they got away from the others.

"If Colonel MacEnroe were here, son, you wouldn't have an ass left, would you?"

"I don't . . ."

"Man, you're in hostile territory and you're top dog here. You're letting yourself be pushed around and jollied up, Duggs. Drinking whiskey, acting like a damned rookie . . . you got someone watching the horses?"

"Yeah, I do."

"All right. Kick out that other fire and let's roll up and get some sleep."

"The ladies are still sitting around the fire, Mr. Justice. I mean . . ."

"Forget it, Alvin. Tell me this, how in hell'd you ever get those corporal's stripes?"

"You don't have to take on like this, Justice."

"No? Damn you, Alvin, we're in this together. My skin, your skin, the ladies' skins. You make a mistake and it costs me. I know you're a fighter, know you take orders. Now, dammit, learn to give some, learn to think for yourself. If you can't cut it, say so," Justice said. "I'll take charge of your soldiers myself."

"There's no call for that," Alvin said miserably. "I reckon I can handle it."

"Then do it," Justice said impatiently. He turned and walked away. Mr. Justice, he told himself, you do have a knack for making friends.

Both Duggs and Bronk Hodges were mad now. Keep, Cobb, and the women already were. The hell with them all. They could do whatever damned-fool thing they wished, but they couldn't play games with Ruff Justice's life.

He approached the fire that still glowed peacefully beneath the dusk-purpled sky. Sarah Farmer wore a white blouse, divided riding skirt, and a wide-brimmed hat hanging by a string down her back. She sat on a log holding a tin cup of coffee. Across from her were Cobb and Gertrude looking very cuddly and cute together.

Justice hooked the coffeepot out of the fire and poured

himself a cup. Then he sat beside Sarah Farmer without asking or being asked.

"Everyone eat already?"

"Yes." Sarah squeaked a little.

"At least you didn't get up and walk away," Ruff said. He was hunched forward, looking into the fire, liking the gold and scarlet, ever-changing tapestry.

"Why would I do that?" Sarah Farmer asked.

Ruff glanced at her, saw that her eyes, open and curious, were on him. He shrugged. "We never got off to much of a start."

"No, I guess we didn't."

Cobb and Gertrude hadn't said a word. They sat on some sort of canvas-and-wood folding chairs, the coffee in their own cups steaming.

Now Cobb looked up as Alvin Duggs approached the fire. "What is it, Corporal?"

"Got to put the fire out, sir. We should have had our cooking all done by sunset, the fires out after dark. That'll have to be the rule from now on." Alvin slowly kicked dirt onto the fire. He didn't once glance at Ruff Justice. No one likes to be reminded that he's remiss.

Ruff sipped at his coffee, watched as the fire went out. The sky went dark and the stars, big and brilliant, blinked on one by one.

"Will it rain, Mr. Justice?" Sarah asked. She seemed closer in the darkness. He could feel the heat of her body, smell her lilac powder.

"Yes," Ruff said, looking skyward. "It's been holding back, but I think tomorrow we'll get some rain."

"That will be bad for the wagons."

"Yes, ma'am" he told her.

Cobb rose from the other side of the fire ring, cleared his throat, and said, "I think we will be turning in now. It's been a long day."

"Don't let me keep you," Ruff said cheerfully.

"Miss Farmer?" Cobb said with some irritation and a little unwarranted possessiveness.

"I'll be along shortly, Professor."

"Very well. Good night, then."

"Good night," Sarah responded. "Good night, Gertrude."

Gertrude wished her the same and the two scientists went off, arm in arm, marching stiffly to their own very different drummer.

"That's a pair to draw to," Ruff said.

"They are, aren't they?" Sarah laughed. It was a pleasant laugh, soft, musical. Ruff decided he liked it. He decided that he liked Sarah Farmer. The darkness seemed to have taken the hard edges off her, to have softened her.

"Look at that sky," she said with wonder. It was a fine sky, all silver and black and huge, beyond comprehension in its depth and distance. "I can almost see why my father stayed out here."

"It wasn't for the gold?" Ruff asked bluntly.

"Oh, that was a part of it," she said. "Gold for my brother Andy, for me. Pa wanted us to be educated, of course, and he didn't want us to have it as hard as he did when he was a boy down South . . . Well, yes, he wanted the gold, but that wasn't all that kept him in the West. You could tell that from his letters."

"He wrote often, then?"

"No. It was hard for him. Three times in two years." Her voice was wistful. It was as if she were mourning a lost childhood, maybe the hours, the days she never had with her father.

"Your brother was older than you?"

"*Is* older than me," Sarah said firmly. "He's not dead, nor is Father."

"You've got to realize . . ."

"They are not dead. I don't know what happened to

them, but they are not dead. That is that." Her voice
was brisk but firm.

Ruff shrugged in the darkness. You couldn't argue
with that sort of logic. However, if the Farmers, father and son, were alive out here after this length of
time, it was nothing short of miraculous.

He said nothing like that to Sarah. "How did you
come to meet Mr. Keep anyway?" he asked instead.

"He came looking for me. He knew that my father
and his brother were partners with some other men in
a mining operation out here. He was worried about
his brother and meant to come west to look for him."

"And he invited you along."

"Yes, he did. I agreed because of the professor and
Gertrude. I wouldn't have come alone with Mr. Keep,
of course."

"How did he come to tie up with them anyway?"

"Well, after receiving the diary, Mr. Keep went to
the Ohio university where Professor Cobb teaches. He
wanted to find out something about the Stone Warriors,
as they were called in the diary. Well, the long and
short of it is that the professor became so interested
that he trailed along, sponsoring us, actually, through
the Department of the Interior."

"All very fortuitous for Mr. Keep."

"Pardon me?"

"Nothing, Miss Farmer, nothing. I've lived an evil
life and I tend to look for the evil in other men."

"And the women?"

"Are there evil women?" Ruff asked lightly.

"Not with this party," Sarah answered, trying to
match his tone.

"No. Not with this party," Ruff Justice said, and the
timbre of his voice deepened, sent a chill up Sarah
Farmer's spine.

She rose abruptly, too abruptly. "It's getting cold.
I've got to turn in, Mr. Justice."

"Yes."

Still she stood there in the night, saying nothing for a long minute before she brushed past him, turned her head back to say, "Good night, Mr. Justice." Then she walked away, her arms folded beneath her breasts, her back straight, her hips moving deliberately, not provocatively by intention, but with the knowledge that his eyes were on her, watching.

Ruff walked back through the darkness to where he had left his horse. There wasn't any conversation in the camp now, just the mumbling and grumbling of men turning in after a hard day. Ruff took the black some distance from the camp and picketed it in the long grass. Then he sat down, rifle across his lap, to look things over, to think.

The sentries were visible as hell against the starry skyline. The campsite itself was in a bad spot, a sort of hollow that might have been a huge buffalo wallow once upon a time, centuries ago. It was easily approachable, practically indefensible. They could only hope that there wasn't a Sioux raiding party within striking range.

Ruff shook out his groundsheet and blanket and rolled up, watching the stars for a long time, listening to his horse crop grass.

He had fallen asleep, dreaming a disconnected dream full of firefalls and black-eyed Indian women, skeletons, and spooks.

He was no longer asleep. Ruff's eyes blinked open and he fought his way to alertness. Something had awakened him and he couldn't figure out what it was. That annoyed and worried him.

Slowly his eyes shifted as his hand dropped to the holstered Colt beside his right thigh. He slipped the gun from its holster and slowly thumbed back the hammer. He saw his horse then and he knew. The big black was against the starry sky like a silhouette pasted there. It was braced expectantly, its ears pricked, alert and wary.

Ruff followed the horse's eyes, still careful not to move suddenly; he would appear asleep unless the starlight on his eyes was seen.

And then Justice saw him. He saw him a moment too late, however; the man hurled himself through the air at Justice, a knife flashing, and Justice fired through the blanket, the pistol shot shattering the night.

As if that shot had ignited a cache of explosives, the world suddenly detonated, the night filling with the roar of gunfire, screams of pain, the thunder of the guns.

The Sioux were pouring into the camp.

# 7

---•——◆——•---

Justice kicked the dead man aside. Falling, his attacker had pinned him to the earth. Now Ruff rolled him away as the camp below exploded with gunfire. Justice saw the horsemen riding through the camp, saw the answering stabs of flame from beneath and behind the wagons. The war whoops were loud in the night.

There weren't many in this raiding party, but then there weren't many of them. Ruff started down the slope at a run, going to his knee to fire the buffalo gun as one of the Indians presented himself and his pony in full silhouette against the sky. The Sioux screamed and went down, to be trampled by his war horse.

Ruff was into the camp now, working his way toward the wagon where the women had been sleeping. An Indian reared up before him, rifle leveled, and was blown back, an agonized yell piercing the night as the big .56 did its work.

Ruff dodged past the downed Sioux and crossed the camp. A spate of rifle fire erupted from beyond the supply wagon, and Justice glanced that way, seeing nothing but the crazed darting of dark figures, the arrows of fire as rifles spoke.

The activity was furious at the women's wagon. Ruff could make out half a dozen warriors on foot assaulting the position, see the answering fire of a single rifle fired from underneath the wagon.

He lent a hand. The .56 spoke twice and two warriors went down, screaming out their pain. Answering shots drove Ruff to his belly, where he reloaded rapidly.

Behind him now fire blazed. The supply wagon had been set on fire and golden sparks splashed against the blue-black skies, illuminating the camping circle.

The rifle beneath the wagon had ceased firing now. Ruff could see the sprawled figure of a man there. Dead or disabled, he was no longer able to answer the attack of the Sioux. The Indians realized that and made their move. Three rifles opened up from the right; Justice heard a woman scream—Sarah or Gertrude Eccles, he couldn't be sure.

One thing he knew: the scream was not a scream of pain, but one of terror. He got to his feet, fired with his revolver in the direction of the Sioux position, and moving in a crouch, dashed toward the wagon.

The canvas top of the wagon smoldered now as drifting sparks from the supply wagon touched it. Justice saw tiny tongues of flame shifting across the top. Simultaneously he saw the figure beneath the wagon, and identified it as one of the soldiers.

He hit the wagon full bore, leaping up the step and into it as the rifle fire at his back splintered the tailgate around him.

The Sioux had Gertrude Eccles by the hair, his free hand tearing at the front of her blouse. His rifle lay on the floor of the wagon, temporarily neglected. That was a big mistake.

Ruff fired from the hip and the Sioux leapt backwards, his face vanishing in a mask of blood. He sagged to the floor of the wagon, to lie twitching as Gertrude Eccles screamed again and covered her eyes with trembling hands.

Ruff saw Sarah Farmer near the front of the wagon fumbling to reload an old .45-70 Springfield. Justice tossed her the Spencer in his right hand and turned to take up a position in the rear of the wagon. He heard the Spencer boom, felt a shuddering Gertrude Eccles crawl up beside him to cling to him as the battle raged.

A bit of smoldering canvas fell down from the roof. Outside, three Sioux on galloping horses rode past, whooping, firing weapons at random.

Justice fired back, but it wasn't randomly. His first bullet tagged a Sioux in the neck and the man was yanked from his horse by the .44-40 bullet. Ruff's second shot was a miss, burning a horse on the withers. The third was a solid hit, tagging a pinto pony behind the shoulder. The animal folded up, somersaulting through the air, throwing its rider free.

The Spencer roared again and suddenly it was silent—the quietest night Justice had ever heard. There was just nothing at all. Then things came back together. He could hear the crackling of fire as the canvas overhead burned, the snuffling of Gertrude Eccles as she lay clutching at him, her little mewling sounds pathetic and childish.

"Get out of the wagon," Ruff called to Sarah Farmer.

"If they're out there . . ."

"It's better than being roasted alive," Ruff shouted back angrily. The canvas top had caught strongly now. Crimson flames danced and writhed along its length. Tongues of liquid flame dropped to the wagon bed and began seeking a hold on the planks.

"Up!" Ruff shouted at Gertrude Eccles.

"No." Her voice quavered. Her hands grasped at Ruff's arm; her eyes were wide and hysterical.

"Up and out, dammit, Gertie." He yanked her to her feet and shoved. "Now!"

"Please, please." She went to her knees clawing at Ruff. Help came from an unexpected quarter.

"That is quite enough," Sarah Farmer said angrily. She snatched the scientist to her feet as flames crackled all around them, illuminating the women's face, lighting their bodies through the nightgowns they wore. "Do you hear me?"

"I can't," Gertrude sniveled.

Sarah's hand flashed forward and Ruff heard the loud crack as she slapped the scientist on the face with force. "Now you can! Get out of this wagon. I'll not be burned alive to please you."

Sarah gave a shove and Gertrude staggered toward the tailgate, whimpering and moaning.

Ruff took his .56 from Sarah's hands and winked at her. "Tough, aren't you?"

She didn't answer. Sarah hoisted her nightgown and leapt for the ground, landing on her feet not far from Gertrude Eccles. Together the two women made a run for the darkness beyond.

Ruff covered them from the wagon until he couldn't make them out anymore, then he too leapt to the ground and crouched staring at the night as great clouds of black smoke billowed into the night sky.

"Ruff?"

"That you, Andy?"

"Yes, sir, it's me."

"What's the score?"

Duggs raced to Ruff's position, keeping low. His face was fire-blackened, his uniform shirt unbuttoned. He shook his head. "Don't know. They seem to be gone. I sent a chase party after them—three men. That's all I got."

"Three soldiers down?"

"Two dead. Ed Buckles with a hole in his leg."

"How about the civilians?" The fire popped loudly behind Ruff and they ducked reflexively.

"Two of the sheepherders. As far as I know, that's it. I haven't seen Keep or Bronk Hodges since it started, though."

"I saw Hodges," Ruff said. "You can scratch him off your list."

Something in Justice's tone caused Andy Duggs to ask, "Something happen between you and Hodges?"

"He tried to kill me, Andy. That's what woke me up. Bronk Hodges tried to stab me in my bed."

"Jesus."

"Yeah." Ruff's eyes were still searching the darkness. The Sioux seemed to be gone, but you couldn't afford to trust to seemed-to-be.

"That business about the whiskey really set him off, did it?" Duggs asked.

"Did it?" Ruff said.

"That was it, wasn't it?"

"You tell me, Andy. Is that enough to kill a man over? To send Bronk Hodges, who hadn't much left, out crawling through the grass to cut my throat with his bowie."

"Why, then?"

"I don't know. I mean to find out, though. Someone put him up to it, I'll wager that. Bronk didn't have the simple ambition to come looking for me even if he was that mad—and I doubt that. He must have expected me to say something about the drinking."

"What a mess," Duggs said sourly. "Maybe this will convince these greenhorns they don't belong out here."

"We can hope so, but I doubt it. Cobb's too determined, Keep and Hallop too damned greedy." Ruff stood. "They'll stick."

"If they're still alive."

"Yes—if they're alive."

Everyone had begun to move—cautiously—to pull

back toward the center of camp. Sarah walked toward Ruff Justice, leading Gertrude Eccles, who was as limp as a rag doll, barely able to keep her feet. Two of the sentries were riding in. One of them, a kid of eighteen, had a bullet through his shoulder and Duggs went to see to him as Cobb, Keep, and Hallop joined the little group. Cobb took Gertrude from Sarah and stood holding her. Without his spectacles, Cobb looked even more round-faced, less competent to exist out here.

"What do we do now?" Hallop asked.

"Stand steady. Stick together," Justice told them. "We can make a little redoubt behind the burned wagons—the supply wagon, I think."

"They'll be back?" Sarah asked, the fear showing through.

"No telling. Probably not," Ruff answered. "Not unless they've got some more people somewhere. They probably got all they wanted here tonight."

"I thought they didn't fight at night," Sarah said. Her voice was merely weary now. She was standing next to Justice and her hands took hold of his arm. She leaned her head against his shoulder.

"You've got to quit believing those dime novels," Justice said. His voice was light, but there was a serious note in it too. You don't make jokes easily with the dead lying around you. "Sure they fight at night. For raiding it's the only time. That was what they wanted, I think—to slip in and snatch our horses, a few blankets, whatever they could find lying around loose. They were a small band, not anxious to mix it up with repeating rifles."

"Then what happened?" Sarah asked. She looked up into his face. Her eyes were bright, her hair highlighted by the fire that still burned.

"I woke up," Ruff said. "Bronk Hodges woke me up, and that was bad luck for Hodges and for the Sioux."

"I want to go back," Gertrude Eccles was saying,

and it was the first sensible thing Ruff had heard the woman say.

"You'll feel better in the morning. Calm yourself now, Gertrude," Cobb answered. "Things will look much better in the morning."

Maybe they would. Ruff doubted it. In the morning they would be burying the dead, looking down into those twisted, gray faces, knowing that it could be any one of them that was being planted.

"Let's tip that grub wagon over on its side," Justice said to Keep.

"All right." Keep was subdued, thoughtful. "You men want to give us a hand?" he asked the remaining sheepherders.

In a minute they had the wagon up and over. Behind them were the cottonwoods and the rising bluff, not the best of defenses, but they would help. Anyone attacking from the front would be in an unhappy position.

"First thing in the morning strip the wagon of foodstuffs," Justice said. "We'll have to get by with the one wagon, but it should do it."

"Justice," Tom Keep said, and Ruff turned to face the little fox, who seemed not frightened by events, but bemused, unhappy. "This isn't going to stop me from going on, so you might as well save your breath— but if you can get the women and Cobb to give it up, maybe you'd be doing us all a favor."

"Maybe. Maybe you're right," Justice said. "We hit Lode tomorrow, maybe we can bid you good-bye from there."

"Maybe. She's got you fooled, hasn't she, Justice?"

"Who?"

"Sarah Farmer, dammit! You know who."

"Maybe she has. What are you talking about now?"

"The gold, Justice," Keep hissed. "You think she wants to find her brother and father? That's a laugh, isn't it? No sane person would expect to find them alive after this length of time. It's the gold she wants, Justice. Nothing would make her happier than to fall over her father's body if he had the gold with him."

"Easy, Keep," Ruff warned him.

"You think I'm kidding you? Just because she's young and attractive? How many young and beautiful ones have you known, Justice, how many that were cats? I tell you she wants the gold, all of it, and if she sees a chance to eliminate me for my share of the claim, she'll damn sure take that, too. I know, Justice, believe me. If you think I'd turn my back on her, you're mad. Good advice, well meant," he added hurriedly.

Ruff glanced over his shoulder. The women, in Cobb's company, were approaching their position. They had had time to dress now, but their hair was still down, loose, hurriedly brushed.

A cat. Ruff leaned on the wagon wheel and looked at her. Hell, Keep was insane. She was young and frightened and desirable. Ruff was certain that Sarah was sincere about finding her family. What game was Keep playing, then?

Easy enough to figure: he wanted Sarah Farmer left behind so that he would have the claim to himself.

"What are you thinking?" Sarah stood in front of him, looking up, her own arms resting on the upturned wagon wheel. Her eyes were shining and her mouth was pursed in curious amusement.

"Thinking about cats," Ruff answered.

"Cats?"

"That's not important. Think you and Gertrude could make some coffee for us?" The fire didn't matter anymore tonight. Everyone within sound of those gunshots knew they were there.

Duggs was counting heads. "Six men altogether, Ruff. Three soldiers—Ed Buckles died—and three sheepherders. I've another with a hole in his shoulder."

Duggs shook his head. "Hard bit of luck. We haven't even reached the badlands yet. I don't suppose the civilians are going to change their mind."

"I haven't seen any sign of it. I'm going to work on them, though," Ruff said. "You've got your men posted?"

"Yes."

"Might as well bring them in, I think. Keep all of our guns together."

"Whatever you say." Duggs shrugged. He didn't look so cocky now. Only very young and very worried. "I guess I didn't handle this too well."

"You did your best." Ruff slapped him on the shoulder and walked away. He found the wounded soldier and stopped to talk with him a minute, telling him, "You're a lucky man, my friend. Tomorrow we'll hit Lode. They've got a hotel there. I think the army's going to have to put you up for a while. I'd rather be doing that than romping through the badlands looking for giants."

"Maybe you would," the soldier said with a pain-inspired grimace. "Maybe *I* would, if I didn't have a hole in my shoulder, Mr. Justice. Right now I just don't give a damn."

"You'll make it." They exchanged a few more words and Ruff left, walking to the upturned wagon, where the smell of boiling coffee met him.

Hallop was standing on the far side of the fire, sipping coffee from a tin cup, his hat tugged low, his hip cocked to one side. Ruff couldn't figure him out, not at all. He wore those two guns like he knew what they were for, yet he was silent for the most part, content to let Keep do the talking. What was Hallop, anyway, insurance for Gregory Keep?

"Here you are."

Sarah handed Ruff a cup of coffee, which he took with thanks. "How's Gertrude?"

"Oh, she's all right," Sarah said with a shrug. "She

and Cobb want to go out and examine the Sioux bodies tomorrow."

"They do, do they? Tell them the Indian dead won't be there tomorrow."

Sarah's eyes opened wide. She tensed, looked past Ruff's shoulder and then into his eyes. "You mean that? Then they're out there, they're out there now?"

"They're out there recovering their dead. That's one reason I pulled the sentries back."

"But they could attack again."

"They won't."

"How can you know?"

"It's an honorable truce. They know I'm giving them the night to take their dead home, to give them a proper funeral."

"I don't understand that. I can't understand this kind of war. What is it, a huge game? You die for the game."

"The losers die," Ruff answered. "It's not a game, it's a way of life to the Sioux. The white man never did understand that, and that's one reason why he'll win. His rules involve total destruction."

"And what about you? What rules do you play by, Mr. Justice?"

"My own. I'm outside the rules."

"No one is, you know," she said.

"Then I *think* I am—and in the end that's the same thing."

"You're a curious animal, Mr. Justice." She was closer to him now, examining him closely, very closely for the first time. "I don't understand you a bit. At first I thought you were just *impossible*. Now I think you're just highly unlikely."

"Maybe. Sarah, have you thought about bailing out? About giving it up. We'll make the little town of Lode tomorrow and it would be a good place for you to—"

"Is that what you and Gregory Keep were talking

about?" she interrupted hotly. "I saw you with your heads together. What did he do, offer you a part of his claim? My part?"

"He didn't offer me anything, lady. I'm not thinking of Keep; I'm thinking of you. This is bad business. Tonight ought to underline that for you."

"Yes, it does underline things," Sarah went on, still hotly. "That I can't afford to trust anyone. I started out to do something, Mr. Justice, and I intend to do it. You are being paid by the army to do a job, not to hinder us from reaching our goal."

Ruff was standing there sipping at his coffee, a smile playing on his lips. That infuriated Sarah Farmer, and her eyes sparked and danced as she spoke.

"Nor will I let the Indian attack run me off. We expected to meet Indians, didn't we? Besides, once we reach the badlands, the Sioux will not attack, will they? We've been told time and again that they won't enter the badlands, that the place is anathema to them."

And that alone, Ruff Justice thought, should have been enough to scare a normal person out of pursuing this course. The Sioux don't scare easy; they may be frightened of different things than a white man, things they don't quite understand might unnerve them a little . . . but fear, stark cold fear was just about unknown in a people that lived by war, warred to live. Anything that struck fear in the heart of the Sioux touched Ruff Justice with more than a little uneasiness.

# 8

———··◆◆◆◆◆··———

Lode, Dakota Territory, was the nearest settlement to the badlands, the last outpost of civilization on the plains. It wouldn't have been there at all, had no reason to exist, but as its name indicated, there had been a gold strike there once. A gold strike that brought them stampeding in from the East, willing to believe anything, to buy maps and equipment, to sacrifice everything they might have had back home in the apparent belief that if a man gets far enough away from where he starts, all things are possible.

Nothing seemed to be possible in Lode.

The one good claim that had started the town sustained it now. A corporation had taken over the operation and it managed to show a small, diminishing profit. Lode survived as an adjunct to the mine, a place where the miners, fewer of them each month, could buy new shoes and rotgut whiskey and lose their pay at the faro tables.

There wasn't much to see of Lode. A row of flimsy false-fronted buildings along one side of the street: general store, saloon, hotel. Farther along was the sheriff's office and jail, which had been dynamited out of solid-rock bluff, then walled up in front to form a very secure and uncomfortable prison.

Up the foothills were the mines, such as they were. The big one was called Western Dakota; the others were all little scratch mines where men dug for a dream.

The party swung down in front of the hotel. The rain had begun falling earlier in the day. Now, isolated showers fell from rolling dark skies. Thunder bellowed from time to time up the canyons.

"It'll settle in good by nightfall," Justice told Sarah. "It's going to be a bad night for travel. Maybe you ought to plan on spending the night here."

"Is Keep planning on spending the night here?"

"Not that I know of."

"Then I won't either. Why are you so anxious to get rid of me, anyway, Mr. Justice?"

Ruff didn't bother to answer. With Alvin Duggs, Justice got the wounded soldier into a hotel bed, got the local barber to come over and have a look at his wounds, paid the clerk, and told him, "It'll be a week or so before we're back. If he can't travel by then, don't throw him out. The army's standing for whatever it costs."

"Yeah?" The clerk was a little suspicious.

"Don't trust the government?" Duggs asked.

"Do they trust me?"

"You've got a point." Duggs laughed. "Anyway, don't skimp. Give the man good hot meals, won't you?"

"Same as I'd do for any wounded man, Corporal."

"That's all I can ask."

Ruff put in, "Don't let the barber stick leeches on him—the man's got a fear of them."

"You'll have to tell the barber that. He favors them."

They told the barber, who looked disappointed. "Best thing in the world for you," he told them earnestly.

"Just lay off them, the kid doesn't like them."

"All right." The barber looked unhappily at his fruit jar full of fat purple leeches.

Outside, it was really starting to come down, lightning arcing across the sky. Ruff and Duggs splashed across the muddy street to the dingy, dark restaurant. The others were seated along a plank table, speaking in low voices. The conversation tailed off rapidly as Justice came in.

"Coming down," Justice told Keep. "You're planning on staying here tonight, I hope."

"No." Keep was adamant. "With what we know? In a gold town? We'd have half the men in Lode following us out in the morning."

"They can't know about the gold."

"I'm not taking any chances."

Ruff's eyes narrowed. He looked at Keep and then at the others. They all seemed in perfect agreement, Cobb, Sarah Farmer, Rupert Hallop. They all thought it was a perfectly delightful idea. It was a good night to try riding rough country, especially driving a wagon.

"Hell, maybe I'm the crazy one," Justice said to Duggs.

"I've slept wet before," Duggs said with a shrug.

"So have I, but I can't say I ever liked it."

Ruff had time to eat and gulp down several cups of coffee before going out again. The wind was gusting up the street, a cold, sheeting wind. Rain fell intermittently. It was an hour before dusk but black as sin. The saloon across the street already had its lanterns lit.

"Ready?" Keep called to Justice.

"Not much."

Keep laughed, helped Sarah up onto the wagon seat, and walked to his own horse. Then they were on their way again, riding out of a deserted town into a deserted dark world.

The wind lifted Ruff's hat brim, pushing it back. It

toyed with the long mane of his big black horse, drove the rain against his body. He had his black rain slicker on now, but it did little to keep out the chill.

The wagon wasn't going to be traveling far or fast on this night. It was just a matter of waiting. It happened a mile on as they tried to ford a black creek running wild across a black land.

The wagon tilted up, lightning painting it vivid white for a moment, and then went over. Ruff heeled his horse forward, swung to one side, and got his rope on the tailgate. "Get on the front wheel," Justice shouted to Duggs.

The soldier had a loop formed and had tied onto the wheel in another second. Two women, very wet, very mad, their skirts heavy with water, were crawling from the creek.

Ruff laughed out loud, and thunder answered his roar of amusement.

"Let's right it, Andy," he called and he walked the big black gelding away, drawing his line tight, pulling until slowly the wagon righted itself and was driven to the far side of the creek, its contents scattered across the creek and strewn about the interior.

"Well?" Ruff was beside Greg Keep. The rain slanted down into their faces. When the lightning flashed again, it showed an expression Ruff didn't care for. The foxy little man had let it all out, perhaps believing no one could see him in the darkness. His expression was hateful, savage, bitter. There was a little wolf in the fox. When he replied to Ruff, however, his voice was calm.

"We'd better camp. Should have stayed in Lode. Sorry."

"It doesn't hurt my feelings any," Ruff said. "The willows over there will shelter us some."

"All right."

"We can post a sentry on the back trail if you're

worried about being followed, though it would take a madman to follow us out tonight."

"Enough gold," Keep said, "will make any man crazy."

"Yeah. Maybe so," Ruff said, and Keep's head turned toward him in the darkness. They looked at each other, although they couldn't see much, just the lines of a face, the shape of a hat against the dark sky. Ruff hadn't forgotten. He hadn't forgotten that Bronk Hodges had tried to knife him in his sleep—and Bronk had never had the ambition to think of that sort of thing for himself.

Someone had set Bronk on him, and Keep was as good a choice as anyone for that role.

Back among the willows they had started making camp. They had started a fire to try to dry everyone out, but there wasn't much point in it with the rain falling like it was. The wind shook the willow brush, shredded the rapidly moving clouds overhead.

Ruff swung down and led his black into the camp, his shoulders hunched, his hat tugged low. It was going to be a bad night.

It was long and cold. The women slept in the wagon and the men rolled up in wet blankets; the wind was cutting, and the rain was hammering down. There was no way to stay warm enough to sleep, and Justice gave it up an hour before dawn.

He started a fire with bits of dry tinder peeled from the inside of a willow bark, and sat on his haunches, watching the gray skies. He prodded the fire to life and soon had a smoky hatful of flame hot enough to boil coffee. He nestled the pot in next to the coals and then suddenly leapt back.

Sparks flew out of the fire and simultaneously the thunder sounded. But it wasn't the thunder of the fall storm. It was a gun that had spoken.

Justice leapt away from the fire, grabbing for his

Colt. He was alone in the camp. The others slept, the cold night dragging slowly past.

He was alone and someone had taken a shot at him. Coffee trickled from the hole in the side of the coffeepot. Steam rose against the darkness.

Justice circled away from the riverside camp, creeping through the stormy night. He wasn't even sure where the shot had come from. The coffeepot had been kicked into the air, changing position. There was no way to mark the sniper's position.

High ground, he thought. It had to be high ground. And the only high ground was on the bluffs across the river. Justice worked that way. Conditions were impossible: the clouds scudded low across the land, darkness smothered the landforms. By the time Ruff reached the bluff, there was no one there, if there ever had been.

The rain had begun again, pouring down to obliterate whatever tracks there might have been. He found only one item—a .44-40 casing, shiny, half-hidden in a clump of chia. Ruff picked it up and fingered it, looking down toward the dark, silent river, back toward the distant town of Lode.

"Any idea who?" Alvin Duggs asked later when Ruff showed him the cartridge.

"Regis Cavanaugh? Who else?"

"You don't sound sure."

"I'm not sure, dammit. It fits his pattern, but it could be anyone. Who doesn't want me here? Why? It gets a little confusing, Duggs. It could be Keep, Hallop— hell it could be you."

"Me?" Duggs laughed. "What the hell would I gain from it, Mr. Justice?"

"Gold. Keep was right about one thing. He said enough gold makes madmen out of us all."

"Not me, Mr. Justice. The idea's plain crazy."

"Is it? Where are you from, Duggs? Where'd you live before army days?"

"I can't see that it makes any difference."

"Probably not. Where?" Ruff demanded.

"Ohio." Duggs turned his eyes down and sipped at his coffee.

"Anywhere near where the Farmers lived or the Keeps?"

"No. Of course not. Christ, Justice, you serious, or what?" Duggs was incensed. Good—let him lose his temper. A man reveals a lot of himself when he's mad.

Duggs got control over his emotions and grinned. 'Hell, there's a lot of people out of Ohio, Justice."

"I reckon."

"Sure. A lot of them."

Half an hour later they were on the trail again. Justice split out from the rest of the party, wanting to be alone to think things over, to study the land ahead of them. The clouds still caked the sky, but they were silver-white, not black, and no rain had fallen for an hour.

The rills ran silver through the badlands ahead of them, merging to form the Little Missouri, which wound through the broken hills, the deep-cut coulees, the washes, and the forbidding canyons. There was little growth here, only cedars scattered along the hilltops, pine and scarce spruce elsewhere, oak and cottonwood in the bottoms, with here and there dense thickets of willow and blackthorn crowding the riverbanks.

Justice sat a low sandy knoll watching the wagon and its escort creep into the tangled, broken land. He could see the windswept, grassy plains behind them, a distant dark stain that might have been a wandering buffalo herd.

They no longer had to worry about the Sioux, he reflected. They would not come here, nor would the

Cheyenne. They were too wise to ride here in quest of mere gold.

As for the claim jumpers Keep feared, Ruff saw no sign of them. His conviction had always been that no one in Lode could know that they were looking for a lost strike. Why had Keep been so certain that someone would be following them?

Justice started the black down toward the river bottom, negotiating a steep sandy bluff. The wind still gusted, chanting through the canyons, and from time to time it could be heard to speak. Deep, nearly animal sounds, chilling moans, screeching warnings—it was, Ruff reminded himself, the land of the Stone Warriors, and whether it was imagination or not, there was an evil feel to the land, a taste to the wind that he was not comfortable with.

He let his black drink its fill at the river, which ran slate gray and white now with the stimulus of the freshets.

Half an hour later he rejoined the party, which had slowed to a walk as it crept up the long, jagged white canyon toward the hills beyond.

"Find something?" Ruff asked Duggs.

"No, but he's sure as hell looking," the corporal said, nodding toward Gregory Keep, who rode at a creeping walk, his eyes searching each crevice and narrow arroyo, each clump of nopal cactus, sage, and greasewood.

He was looking, all right. Looking for gold. And when he found it, what, then?

They had to keep to the riverbed as long as they continued to use the wagon, and Ruff didn't like it down low like that. From the bluffs they could be spotted easily, easily ambushed.

"You don't really expect to be attacked, do you?" Sarah asked. "You don't seriously believe in the Stone Warriors."

"Don't I?"

"It's impossible, that's only an old Indian myth."

"Ask the professor," Ruff said.

"But it can't . . ." She shuddered and fell silent, her eyes searching the brush-clotted sandy canyons around them. "Well, all the same, we've got modern weapons. What could they have to fight with?"

"Your brother and father had modern weapons. It didn't help them."

"They're not dead."

"All right. They're not dead. They just never came out of the badlands."

"Sometimes I don't like you, Ruff Justice," Sarah said petulantly.

"You're entitled. Sometimes I don't much like myself."

"Is this a private conversation?" Rupert Hallop asked, riding up briskly, his horse's hooves spraying damp sand.

"Growing rapidly less private," Ruff answered.

"What about camp, Justice? All right to spend the night in the bottom here?"

"I wouldn't risk it," Ruff answered. "You'd get by with it nine out of ten times, but the tenth you're liable to be riding a flash flood down out of here."

"That's what I thought you'd say." Hallop removed his hat and wiped his brow. "I've been keeping an eye open for a bench or a trail up to the bluffs. Guess I'd better make a serious effort. It'll be dark in a couple of hours."

"I would," Justice said. "If we could talk everyone into abandoning this wagon, it would make it a hell of a lot easier."

"I don't mind, I'm sure," Sarah said. "I don't ride that well, but . . ."

"Uh-uh," Hallop said. "It's got Keep's mining gear in it, got the professor's stuff. They want the wagon."

"It's going to be a slow trail," Ruff said.

Hallop shrugged as if it were none of his concern. Ruff touched his hat to Sarah Farmer and rode off ahead once more, trying to scout the trail through the maze of broken canyons, uptilted, twisted hills. The wagon, he decided, would have to go no matter what Keep and Cobb wanted. The horses could be broken to carry packs, which could be made up out of the wagon top.

Ruff climbed up out of the sultry canyon bottom to sit his horse atop the bluff. He swung down and walked along the rim a way, looking down the sheer slope where pine and red cedar grew.

It was there that he found the footprint.

There was just the one and Ruff had to crouch down low and tilt his head to change the angle of light slightly before he could be sure he was seeing what he thought he was.

It was there, on the sandy earth among the yellowish boulders that clustered together along the rim at this point, where wind-twisted cedars overhung the rim of the canyon bluff.

One single, huge, bare footprint.

No moccasin, no boot. Just foot, human foot, with the toes splayed—perhaps from walking barefoot all his life. An Indian's toes tend to get that way from wearing soft moccasins, Ruff knew. But not like this. Besides, he had never seen an Indian with feet this size.

It was far from comforting.

He knew all about the Stone Warriors, had heard the stories, the theories, the speculation, but he had never seen one, nor did he know of anyone who had. The track before Ruff did something to bring the Stone Warriors forward from the mists of myth, and it was an uncomfortable feeling.

He worked his way down the bluff, clambering hand over hand for fifty feet or so, searching for overturned stones, plants uprooted by a climbing man, another footprint—but there was nothing at all.

Neither could he find anything along the rim, farther back among the trees.

It was nearly dark when he gave it up. The western skies were charcoal, streaked with burnt orange. There was nothing below but badlands as far as the eyes could see, deep in shadow now, ominous, twisted landforms.

And from somewhere very far away came a deep moaning sound—wind-distorted, unidentifiable, savage. It rode the wind, keening higher for a moment before dying away, smothered by wind sounds, by the constant shriek of gusting breezes in the long canyons. Justice stood there for a minute longer, then stepped into leather, his face set and grim. He started the horse down the trail, the moaning still echoing in his ears, striking atavistic chords in his mind.

Ruff rode back toward the night camp deep in thought, every sense alert and jumpy. The camp was easy to spot. The fire was visible from a half-mile away. They apparently felt all danger was past, with the Sioux having been left behind. Justice was far from easy in his own mind. There was the incident of the sniper that morning, the attempted murder by Bronk Hodges . . . and there was the footprint.

When Ruff rode up onto the bench where the night camp had been made, they were all there, gathered around the dead man.

# 9

They seemed to hardly notice Justice when he rode up. They stood around the broken pile of bones, their faces firelit, fire-shadowed, stunned. They formed a weird montage, as if some spell had touched them, holding them mute and motionless.

Gregory Keep broke the spell. "Look at that! There must be a hundred ounces in those two sacks alone. Pure dust. Look at it."

"It doesn't matter that he died, does it?" Sarah Farmer said angrily. "It doesn't matter a bit."

"I knew my brother was dead before I started out," Gregory Keep said. His fox eyes were alert and glittering. "I'm not fool enough to think someone could last out here all this time, Miss Farmer."

"If you think you can hurt me . . ."

"I don't think anything," Keep snapped back. "I'm just telling you that I adjusted to my brother's death a long time back. I didn't come looking for him; I came looking for what he left me, for what he wanted me to have—and I never made a secret of it. Don't look at me that way, lady. At least I'm not a hypocrite, pretending to look for graves when all I want is gold."

"How dare you!" Sarah sounded genuinely shocked, disgusted. "How can you insinuate any such thing, Mr. Keep?"

"What's going on here?" Ruff wanted to know.

Professor Cobb turned toward him, his round pink face glossed by firelight. "Tom Keep—they've found his bones. Or what's left of them."

"You're sure it's Keep?"

"His brother is, and he should know. He recognized the gun Tom Keep carried, the belt buckle."

"He had his gold with him still?"

"That's right. They didn't even take it," Cobb said with excitement. "You know what that means?"

"I think so."

"It means that whoever killed him didn't know what gold dust was, what value it could possibly have," Cobb went on excitedly.

"The bones," Gertrude Eccles said. She was nearly as worked up as the professor. They stood close together, virtually trembling with the thrill of it. "The bones—crushed to fragments. Every single bone in his body. We're close, Mr. Justice, very close."

"Too damn close," Ruff muttered. He didn't mention the footprint. Not now.

He stepped up beside Sarah and slipped an arm around her waist before she realized he was there. She glanced at him, startled, then relaxed in his grip.

Keep was on the ground beside a canvas-covered, shapeless lump. Before him were two canvas sacks of some size. A bit of gold dust glittered in his hand as the firelight reached out and touched it. It glittered prettily, and Ruff, glancing around, saw that there were eyes shining as well. Eyes as bright and dully gleaming as the gold. The soldier to Duggs' right stared with open awe at the gold dust. Why wouldn't he? That was thirty years' soldiering in one lump. The bulky, black-bearded sheepherder behind Hallop had come over from Spain to look for wealth in this land of plenty. He had just set eyes on it. His eyes were hungry and said so. Other eyes weren't so readable, like Cobb's or Hallop's, like Alvin Duggs'.

"You ought to get him underground," Ruff Justice said. "There's sicknesses that cling to the unburied dead. Besides, it's not proper."

"Yes," Keep said, as if coming out of a trance. "You're right, of course, Justice."

"Not here," Sarah Farmer said plaintively. "Not if we're going to camp here."

"We'll take him back down the trail," Ruff said. "We can cave one of these sandy bluffs in over him."

"I wanted to examine him," Cobb said excitedly. "If we can discover . . ."

"What are you, a goddamned ghoul?" Alvin Duggs demanded with unexpected vehemence. "Leave the dead be."

Cobb took an involuntary step backward. "I'm sorry," he stuttered. "I didn't realize . . . Of course I wouldn't want to do anything that might be construed as offensive."

"I don't want you going over him either," Gregory Keep said. He rose, holding a gold sack in each hand. "The corporal's right, leave the dead be. Let them have their silence, their peace."

"But not their gold?" Sarah Farmer asked.

"No." Keep shook his head. "They've got no use for that, Miss Farmer. Me, I do have a use for it. Rupert? You want to take my brother off down the trail and bury him proper?"

"Sure, Mr. Keep."

"I'll give you a hand," Ruff said.

He released Sarah Farmer, who was pale and shaken, no doubt both from the argument and from the finding of the dead man, reminding her that her own brother and father could very well be found next.

Ruff and Hallop went down the trail, dragging their grisly burden. Neither of them spoke as they pushed what was left of Tom Keep over the side and caved in the bank.

"Poor bastard," Hallop said finally. "I guess that's what's in store for all of us in the end."

"That's it," Ruff said. "There's no other way out." They started back toward the campfire. "What's your cut of the gold, Hallop?" Ruff asked unexpectedly.

"I don't get you." The big, craggy gunman looked over at Justice, his expression blank.

"You're with Keep. What's your cut of the gold he found, of the claim he thinks he's going to find?"

"I'm working for wages." Hallop shrugged. "Fifty a month."

"That's not much. Not with all the gold around."

"No." Hallop paused. "I guess it ain't. How much do you make, Mr. Justice? How interested are you in the gold? Me, I make do. Greedy folks get dead sooner than others, I learned that a while back."

"That is true, my friend," Ruff agreed.

"And then, who knows how much gold there is anyway? Keep found himself a little pile today, enough to allow a man a few good times, a few years of high living. But it ain't really enough, is it? Not for the good life."

With that, Hallop was gone, leaving Ruff with the distinct impression that he had been warned—warned that if, or when, they found the strike itself, Hallop would make his play.

How? Justice wondered, watching the back of Hallop as he walked toward the fire. How do you make your play if you're a man alone?

The answer was simple. Maybe Hallop wasn't alone. There was someone on their trail, someone who sniped, who had almost killed Ruff Justice. And who had hired Regis Cavanaugh in the first place? It almost had to have been Hallop.

The camp was silent. The gold or the corpse, the land itself and its eerie sounds, tortured landscapes, heavy breathless air had subdued their spirits—cast a spell over them, one might say.

The soldiers were at the fire filling up for their night watch. The sheepherders were out there now, standing guard while they ate. Gertrude and the professor sat together as always, sharing whatever secrets they had. Ruff poured a cup of coffee and took it with him to the mouth of a shallow wash, where he sat against the cool sand, staring down at the fire in the night.

"You weren't hungry?" Sarah asked.

"No. Not now."

She sat down beside him, drawing up her knees, folding her arms around them. "I hate this," she said unexpectedly, "suddenly hate it."

"It's finding the bones."

"Maybe. It's this land. I don't like the feel of it."

"Nor do I," Ruff admitted.

"Seriously?" She looked at him with surprise. "You aren't afraid. You don't believe . . ."

Ruff debated telling her about the footprint, but decided to keep it to himself. Sarah was frightened already; she didn't need any more unsettling news.

They sat together in the silence, listening to the wind chant and moan, watching the fire blaze away. "I wish I were home," she said. "I mean that—tonight. I wish I were home."

"But you wouldn't consder going?"

"No," Sarah said with determination. "I've come to do something and I'll do it or bust."

"The gold's not what's keeping you at it, is it?"

"The gold."

"Yes. That's what Keep wants. Hallop, I think. It's been suggested that you want the gold."

"Who suggested that?"

"Is it true?"

There was too long a pause. "No, of course not."

She leaned her head against Ruff's shoulder then, and if it was meant to distract him, it worked. He felt a warmth begin to crawl up his spine, flood his groin, lift his pulse higher. He sipped his coffee, put his arm around Sarah Farmer's shoulder, and sat there in the darkness and silence for a long while. She was soft and warm against him, contouring her body to his, soft and affectionate suddenly . . . much like a cat. Wasn't that what Keep had called her? A cat.

After the fire was out and Sarah was sleeping in the wagon with Gertrude Eccles, when the silver moon was riding high in a cloud-stained sky, they came.

Justice lifted his head. He sat there in the awesome silence listening, feeling something. He stared at the camp below the wash where he had sat talking to Sarah Farmer, where he had made his bed.

His hand automatically lowered to the butt of his holstered Colt. It rested there as his eyes scoured the night. He saw nothing, no one. A few vague outlines delineating the bluffs, the hills around them, the smudge of shadow that was the wagon.

That was all. No sentry, no men moving about the camp, not even the silhouette of the broken oak above him.

But he knew.

Justice got to his feet and moved softly down the sandy slope toward the wagon, his heart hammering, the gun in his hand cool and comforting.

He stopped and dropped to a crouch. Near the wagon—or was that imagination? One of the women slipping out to take care of personal business?

He held perfectly still, every sense straining, alert.

Nothing. He saw nothing else and began to move forward again. The wind was groaning in the canyons, sending a chill up Ruff's spine.

The wagon was above him now, stark and murky against the background of rolling sky and dark hills. Justice took another step and the thing rose up from the ground to launch itself at him.

The bulky, demonic thing collided with Ruff's body and they went down together in a heap, Ruff's pistol flying free as they hit the earth together, the thing mauling him, clawing and pawing, panting as they rolled across the ground and slammed into the wagon wheel.

Ruff felt the horny hands at his throat and he brought a knee up hard, driving it into his attacker's groin. A muffled grunt of pain sounded near Ruff's ear, but the hands held their grip.

Justice was beginning to feel it now. The blood supply to his brain was being cut off. The single visible star multiplied itself and became a hundred, a thousand stars of different colors spinning brightly through the void behind his eyes.

Ruff got his right arm free and slammed his forearm against the nose of the man, the thing on top of him, driving it down again and again until bone cracked and hot blood spewed out over his face and the beast fell back with a roar of rage and pain.

Justice reached behind his belt and hooked his bowie from its sheath, slashing out angrily as the monstrous shadow over him started forward again.

Steel met flesh and another roar of pain rolled through the night. Someone was coming on the run from across the camp now, Justice heard a shout of warning. His knife flicked out again, and again there was a cry of pain. The attacking thing stopped, backed away, its deep-throated growling still sounding.

Someone had lighted a torch, and as the fire flared

up, the thing, the man, turned and fled, leaping from the bench where the campsite had been laid to the deep shadows of the canyon below.

Justice was on his feet in a single, pantherish move, following his assailant to the sandy rim of the bench, staring down into the black void at his feet, hearing nothing, seeing nothing.

"What the hell was that?" Gregory Keep demanded.

"Nothing."

"Nothing, hell! I saw you fighting something, someone."

"I don't know who it was," Ruff said wearily.

"There was just the one?" Keep held a torch and by that light Ruff examined the ground around them, searching for tracks. Unfortunately the soft sand didn't take impressions well. There was one imprint that might have been a bare foot, a very large bare foot—or it might not have been. Maybe the night, the dark aura of the place was playing tricks on Ruff's mind. All tracks look larger in sand anyway.

"Just the one," Ruff said, and that, he thought, had been plenty.

"Ruff!" Sarah Farmer was out of the wagon and to him, throwing herself into his arms. She was soft and warm in the night, her hair loose and sleek down her slender back. "I was so frightened. I felt something . . . What happened?"

"Nothing at all. Everything's all right," he said.

"You're lying to me, I know that. I felt—I can't explain it. I felt evil. Was it Indians? Or . . ."

"It was nothing," Justice said again. "Keep, we don't have much use for that torch anymore," he commented sharply, and Keep, shrugging, walked away. Two of the soldiers were there watching, wanting to know as Sarah wanted to know.

They were all unwilling to believe it, all half-convinced already that they knew the truth: that something not quite human, indestructible, massive, and totally evil was walking these badlands.

The soldiers walked away and Sarah was left with Ruff, her fingers plucking at his sleeves, her body still pressed close against his, her breasts moving, generous, warm against him.

Gertrude Eccles was staring at them from behind the canvas wagon flap, her eyes wide, her braided hair hanging loose, her gaze myopic, confused without her bifocals.

"Go on to bed," Ruff said to Sarah. "Your partner there's worried about you."

Gertrude withdrew in a snit.

Sarah laughed. "I'm worried about me too," she said. She still hadn't left Ruff's arms. He was aware of the thinness of the nightdress, of the warmth of her, the soapy scent of her body. "I'm worried about you, all of us." She began to shudder suddenly and Ruff realized she was crying, silently, deeply sobbing. Her strength, the ability to pretend, had suddenly given out and she was only a young, helpless woman in a strange and harrowing land.

"Don't leave me tonight," Sarah said, her eyes anxious and fearful.

"I don't think Gertrude would much care for me staying," Justice said lightly.

"Gertrude can go to hell," Sarah snapped. "If not here, then let me go with you—to your bed."

"You're only frightened, Sarah," Ruff told her.

"I'm frightened, yes. But not *only* frightened. I want to be with you. Do I have to beg?"

"No." Ruff kissed her forehead gently. Then they turned and together walked away from the wagon, crossing the camp, which had again fallen silent, going to the bed he had made in the sandy wash, and there he laid her down.

She was trembling when he pulled off his shirt and

lay down beside her. She was trembling as he lifted her nightgown over her head and placed it aside. She was trembling as his body met hers and he kissed her throat, her breasts, her abdomen, her soft, smooth inner thighs.

"Mr. Justice—please take care of me," she whispered.

"I intend to."

# 10

Sarah Farmer's body—so lushly soft, rounded—disguised an unimagined strength. Beneath the sheathing of feminine flesh was muscle, intent and purposeful. Nature had given her an incredible lithe sureness of joint and sinew, muscle and tendon, a quick, eager strength that met Ruff's own eager competence and matched it with thrusting need, with grasping fingers, searching lips, probing, moist tongue, urgent pelvis.

Her fingers sought his solid, powerful shaft and searched its length, amazed at the maleness of him, wanting to devour and hold him.

She sat up suddenly and threw a leg across him to sit straddling Ruff's hips, her hair brushing his face as she bent down to kiss him, her fingers resting lightly on his shoulders, touching his cheek for a bare moment.

Then she lifted herself, found Ruff's shaft, and positioned him, slowly settling her warmth onto him as the chill night winds blew up the canyon.

She shuddered and leaned forward, Ruff's hands finding her breasts, young, full, warm. Then she began to sway, to move against him, deliberately, slowly at first as if performing some exact, methodical ceremony. Her breath was warm against Ruff's cheek, his eyes, and his lips as she kissed him. Her warm mouth ran in circles around his face, finding his ear, his throat as the cadence of her hips increased, her inner muscles working against Ruff as she lifted herself higher, her breath catching as a spasm of joy washed over her.

Sarah reached between her thighs, and her fingers encircled Ruff, touching him where he entered her. Then, slowly, she settled on him again, her head now thrown back, her breasts standing out proudly, her mouth half-open, eyes half-closed in the starlight.

She swayed against him, trembled. Ruff's hands still mauled her breasts, and that seemed to be all that held her up as she pitched and thrust, her pelvis grinding into his, her breath coming in hard, rapid gasps as Justice, smiling softly, arched his own back and settled himself deeply, feeling his own need rising, feeling the demand of his body as he felt the woman against him—thigh and buttocks, hands and lips, all wanting, hungrily searching, warm and damp and needful. He finished with a rare and deep rush, feeling Sarah's last violent quaking before she collapsed against him with a little sob to lie there, her heart hammering, her lips moving soundlessly against his hard-muscled chest. Ruff stroked her dark hair and watched the sable night run past.

When he awoke, she was gone. There was a hint of gray in the eastern sky and Justice rolled out, feeling stiff and older than he should have. The old bullet holes in his shoulder were acting up this morning, the bits of bone and gristle that had been shot away shifted around irritatingly, painfully within the joint.

He tugged his boots on in the nearly complete darkness, glancing at the skies, which showed no stars now, only angry, boiling clouds filled with cold rain. The rain had begun before he had finished dressing.

He tramped up to the top of the bluff and had a look around as predawn lightened the skies to steel blue and deep gray. There wasn't much to see, just the empty, twisted land running away toward the horizon. But there were no morning campfires in the distances, and that was encouraging.

Keep had been sure that the men of Lode would try to follow them—they weren't. Or they were cold and cautious on this morning, eating breakfast from a can. It wasn't likely for a band of claim jumpers, men acting on impulse.

Regis Cavanaugh would be a different matter. He was a man used to stalking, to hunting quietly, to biding his time until he had line of sight and the high ground.

Ruff went back down, saw to his black, which appeared glad to see him on this chilly damp morning. Then he walked to the camp, where Hallop was hunched over a small fire and one of the sheepherders, a man called Ramón, was frying bacon in a black iron skillet.

" 'Morning," Hallop said.

"Howdy." Ruff crouched down beside Hallop and poured himself a cup of steaming black coffee. It was bitter and bracing.

"We had a little excitement last night," Hallop said.

"Did we?"

Hallop glanced at the man in buckskins and laughed. "Or weren't you wrasslin' with some Indian?"

"I was wrasslin'," Ruff said with a smile, "but it wasn't an Indian."

"No? How do you know?"

"No knife," Ruff said, taking another sip of coffee. And if it had been an Indian, he would be dead by now. No, whoever it was had carried no knife, and to Ruff's mind, that eliminated Indians.

Hallop's curiosity seemed more than incidental, but Ruff couldn't put a handle on the curiosity the gunman exhibited.

After finishing his coffee, he walked to where the struggle had taken place the night before. There wasn't a lot to see, only a hollow gouged in the sandy soil, a few tangled tracks, one of them possibly barefoot—if you used your imagination.

" 'Morning!"

Ruff turned toward the bright voice. Sarah Farmer's head poked from the back of the wagon. Her cheeks were flushed, her dark hair down and loose. She was nearly dressed, wearing a white blouse that was almost buttoned. Ruff walked to her and kissed her good morning.

"How are you?" he asked. He kept his voice low, as Gertrude Eccles was moving about inside the wagon.

"Terrific! How did you think I'd be?"

"Ready to have some breakfast?" Ruff asked.

"If you'll give me a minute."

"Sure."

She kissed him again, quickly, and the canvas flap dropped shut. Gertrude Eccles appeared a few minutes later, and Ruff, thinking it was Sarah, reached up to help her down before he identified the scientist. She recoiled sharply.

"Sorry." Ruff grinned.

"What in the world are you doing?" Gertrude asked. She held a hand to her breast. Her eyes were wide, her colorless lips compressed. "May I get down?"

Ruff waved an arm and bowed, and Gertrude got down, looking cautiously behind her as if afraid Ruff might try to goose her. He watched her walk away, hips swishing, back rigid, head held high, light-brown hair knotted severely.

"Ready?" Sarah appeared and looked down. Ruff took her by the waist and swung her down. She looked toward where Miss Eccles was walking. "Do you like that?"

"It puzzles me, that's all. Puzzles me when a woman wants to act like a man."

"Maybe she doesn't when the professor is around," Sarah suggested with a stifled giggle.

"Maybe not." Ruff kissed her hair, liking the clean, shiny smell of it. "Let's have some coffee, woman."

Together they walked to the fire. Hallop was gone, but Keep was there, looking as if he had passed a sleepless night—maybe he was already worried about protecting his gold dust.

He nodded to Ruff and Sarah without seeming to see them. Professor Cobb and Gertrude stood to one side eating from tin plates, together and apart, as usual.

"We must be within twenty miles of the claim," Keep said almost to himself. His head bobbed up, however, and he looked at Ruff Justice intently. "According to the diary, we're right on course. We cross the Dusty Creek tomorrow where it runs into the Little Missouri."

"Do we?" Ruff asked.

"Well, we should, shouldn't we? It's only twenty miles."

"The miles have a way of getting longer out here," Ruff replied.

"I know what you mean," Keep grunted. He said nothing more, though Ruff thought he wanted to. Justice still hadn't figured Keep out. He seemed so sly, slick, devious, although he hadn't done anything overt.

"Are we ready, Mr. Justice?" Alvin Duggs asked.

Ruff looked up and nodded. "All ready, Corporal." He tossed the dregs of his coffee into the fire to steam and hiss. Ruff looked to the cold, drizzling skies and then back to Sarah Farmer. "It's going to be a rough one."

"That's all right. I'll be thinking of last night—and tonight?"

"And tonight," Ruff agreed.

Justice saddled up and rode out while the rest of the camp packed and hitched and settled down for the day's work. He hadn't gone a mile when he decided that they had a problem. There was just no way for the wagon to cross the big red arroyo in front of them.

Justice sat on the lip of the canyon, the gusting wind cold across his body. Something pale, unnatural drew his eye, and he dismounted and walked down the bluff toward the riverbank. There was a bit of twisted, weather-dried harness; a saddle, ancient, curled at the corners; and the bones of a dead man half-buried in the sandy beach of the tiny creek.

Bones there were, and every one of them broken to splinters. Ruff felt the icy little fingers creeping up his back. He lifted his eyes to the surrounding willow brush, seeing nothing, hearing nothing.

Yet they were there. You could feel it somehow. They were there and they were watching.

Ruff took the purse from the man's vest pocket, looked around a little. Kicking the sand, he revealed a rusted Colt Dragoon pistol and a broken spur. Then he slowly climbed the bluff again.

He rode up beside the wagon, climbed onto the bench, and sat between Gertrude and Sarah. Gertrude complained shrilly, but Ruff ignored her. He handed the purse to Sarah, taking the reins himself as his black loped alongside.

"Recognize it?"

"No." She hesitated. "Should I?"

"I don't know."

Gertrude Eccles interrupted with another shrill complaint.

Justice turned his cold blue eyes on her. "Woman, would you have the decency to shut up for one minute?"

"What's in it?" Sarah asked. She fingered the leather purse, not looking at it, but at Ruff Justice.

"I didn't open it. I figured ... there haven't been that many people in the badlands, Sarah."

"That doesn't mean it's my father's or Andy's."

"No," he agreed, "it doesn't. Have a look, Sarah. Let's not put it off. We need to know, all of us."

With trembling fingers she opened the purse. The paper inside was protected by oilskin. It was evidence of a filed claim, not yet notarized, and wrapped inside of that a letter in a frilly feminine hand.

Sarah dropped the letter and stared ahead, her hand to her lips.

"Is it?"

"Yes." She nodded, closing her eyes. Ruff picked the letter up from the floorboard of the wagon box. It was signed "Sarah, your loving daughter."

"I'm sorry, Sarah."

"It doesn't mean he's dead."

"I found a body."

"But not necessarily his." She was grasping at straws now. Gertrude Eccles looked disgusted with the display of emotion. "I have to see it," Sarah insisted.

"All right. We'll be up on it in half an hour or so. Sarah ... I am sorry."

"I know," she said, and in that moment Ruff knew that she had accepted the fact of her father's death.

Justice kissed her lightly on the forehead, returned the reins to Sarah, and stepped into the saddle of his black, turning it away toward the point of the caravan.

"We're going to have to cut the wagon loose," Ruff told Gregory Keep.

"We'll need it, Justice."

"You might need it, but you can't have it. There's a long arroyo ahead of us, very deep, and there's no crossing—not for miles."

"I've got my gear in that wagon."

"You've known for a long while we couldn't take the wagons all the way in. You'll have to pack it."

"Yeah." Keep sighed. "Well, we can leave it up top here, I suppose—hide it and hope for the best. What were you talking to the woman about, Justice?"

"I found a dead man down below."

"Ansel Farmer?" Keep's eyes brightened.

"Looks like it."

"Tough for the girl."

"Tough," Justice replied.

"There weren't . . . You didn't find any papers with the body, did you?"

"What kind of papers, Keep?"

"Mining claims. I mean, if Farmer filed legally, he'd likely have kept the papers with him. Maybe in his boot or some such. And if he didn't file . . ." Keep had gone too far, and he knew it.

"If he didn't file, then whoever does file owns the whole claim," Ruff suggested, "and to hell with the relatives of Farmer and MacDonald and the rest of them."

"That's not what I was going to say," Keep told him. The look was back—that wolfish little look that revealed a more dangerous Gregory Keep than the man wanted to show. Ruff smiled.

"Sorry. I jump to conclusions sometimes."

"That's all right," Keep replied easily. The two men exchanged a long, understanding glance, and for the first time they admitted the dislike behind the words, the smiles. Gregory Keep was out for gold, and spilling a little blood wasn't going to stop him a bit.

Keep looked again at Justice as if to say, "There—now you know," and then with a quick nod he slowed his horse and fell back to explain about the wagon to Horace Cobb.

The rain hammered down. Lightning flashed against a cold, rolling sky. The wagon was left in a narrow canyon, stripped of its goods and its horses.

Through the mud and slosh they found their way to the river and they clambered down the bank. Ruff's black went to its haunches, sliding to the sandy beach below where the bones lay.

The river rushed by, murmuring, hissing. Sarah Farmer crouched over the pile of bones, the rotted clothing, the tarnished metal.

"Well?" Ruff asked.

"It's his belt buckle. I was with him when he bought it." She turned blank eyes to him. "This is my father."

He didn't look like anyone's father; he wasn't human, or even a thing in human form. The bones were splintered and yellowed, the clothes only rags.

"Let's bury him, Corporal Duggs! All right, Sarah?"

"Yes," she said. She leaned against him, holding his hand tightly as the rain rushed down.

The soldiers got to work. It didn't take long in that sandy soil, and what there was of Ansel Farmer was rolled into the pit.

"What did they do to him?" Gertrude Eccles said in a low voice. "Why would anyone do that to a man?"

The soldiers began shoveling sand back on the body with their camp shovels. Ruff stood aside, hat in his hand, the rain washing down over him. No one knew the words to say, and so they didn't say anything.

He watched the river and then the soldiers. He was watching when the thunder sounded and the soldier beside Alvin Duggs leapt backward, his mouth filling with a blood-choked scream.

"Get down," Justice shouted.

He pushed Sarah to the ground, hurriedly unsheathed his own rifle, and hit the earth, bringing the Spencer up, his eyes searching the dark day, the rain-screened bluffs.

Thunder, hell—that was a rifle shot and the soldier lay dead or dying on the sand behind them.

"Alvin? If he's alive, better get to him quick."

"He's dead, Mr. Justice. Dead," Duggs repeated with shock and dismay. "I couldn't see where the shot came from," he shouted above the roar of the rain, the rushing babble of the river, the wind sounds. "The bluffs? Up near the cedars?"

"I don't know. Just stay down. I'll take a look."

"He's got us pretty well covered, Mr. Justice."

"Yeah." He had them, all right. Covered well enough to pick them all off one by one as they lay flat against the sandy beach. That was the reason someone had to go up there, and Justice figured himself for the best Injun.

"Ruff . . ." Sarah was clutching at his sleeve, wanting to say something. There was just nothing positive she could say or do.

Roughly he told her, "Just keep your head down. Far down."

Then the rifle above them spoke again and Ruff saw the sheepherder take it. The top half of his skull was blown away in a bloody mist. Gertrude Eccles, who was near enough to be spattered by blood, vomited into her hands.

Justice was off and running, weaving toward the bluff. The length of time between shots had to mean something, he thought as he ran. An inexperienced man with a single-shot weapon would have been his first guess, but the man was experienced enough to hit what he aimed at.

There wasn't time for much speculation. Justice heard

the distant crackle of gunfire, felt sand spray up into his face from a near miss.

Three more steps and he was into the tangled mat of brush—willow, manzanita, sage—and climbing. He heard another shot ringing in the canyon, saw a flash of white lightning, then the world was hushed by the falling rain, which smothered everything.

Justice was crawling up through the brush, his eyes alert. Cold water clung to the willow and sage like strands of pearls. The ground beneath him was sandy and soft. In minutes he was atop the bluff, weaving through the trees, eastward, toward the position he estimated the sniper had held. The clouds had lowered their shaggy heads. The tops of the scraggly spruce were cut off by them. The wind whistled mockingly through the trees.

Ruff stopped, panting, his breath steaming from his lips. There was just nothing at all. Nothing to see, no movement: only the wind and the cloud shadows and the constant cold rain.

He moved forward again, eyes shuttling from side to side, probing the weather, the shadows.

Nothing.

He emerged onto the rim and stood looking back toward the river. He could make out the blue of Duggs' uniform, the white of Sarah's jacket, the red scarf around Hallop's neck.

He searched the ground and the brush for some time, but if there had been any signs, the rain had washed them away. The sniper had gotten away again. And how many more people would he kill before Ruff could stop him?

He stood looking out across the canyon toward the cloud-darkened badlands beyond, not liking the situation a bit. Behind them was a kill-crazy sniper, ahead a band of savage murderers. A man with good sense would pull out right now and leave the others to their fate. A man with good sense.

Ruff Justice started down the sandy bluff toward the waiting party.

# 11

"That's it!" Dr. Horace Cobb stood in the driving rain staring with awe at the high-rising red bluffs, the lone, broken pine that marked the ancient trail. "The caves are up there, somewhere."

"Somewhere," Gertrude Eccles repeated. The woman was somewhat subdued, had been since the Sioux attack. She had tasted danger and found it not to her liking. Now she stood beside Cobb studying the twisted, gorge-cut landscape before her.

"Their camp should have been below the pine, near the limestone outcropping."

It was Keep who spoke, and his eyes searched the land around them as diligently as Cobb's. The object of his search was a little different. There was gold here, much gold; and if a man had a chance, if he could survive for a few months, a few weeks, long enough to dredge some of it from the gravel along the streambed, to pan it and wash it and sack it, he would be set for life.

There were women and wine and grand hotels and racehorses and houses and long glittering nights to be had, and the means was so near that Keep could taste it now. He referred to the diary constantly, checking for trail markers, for the bald peak, the broken oak, the lightning-struck boulder. He was sure now that he was in the right area, and his excitement stimulated the others. His and Cobb's.

Cobb was worked up to a fever pitch at the thought of finding the Stone Warrior's cave—he was the only one.

The land rose in a series of convoluted benches and sandy reddish hills from the Little Missouri here. Ruff took Duggs aside and told him, "There's only a few of us to handle this duty, but we'd better handle it right. You, me, the trooper there. One of us had better stay up on the bluffs at all times."

Duggs looked up dubiously. "Tough riding up there, Mr. Justice. No guarantee we'd be on the right side of things. No guarantee we'd be able to do a damn thing if he goes to sniping again."

"No, there isn't." Justice knew that all too well. 'But we've got no chance at all if we're all down here."

"All right." Duggs sighed. "I'll send Chambers up along the west bluff there. It looks like he may be able to keep up with us."

While Duggs went off to inform his last man of his assignment, Ruff rode forward to where Keep, tightening his cinch, was ready to ride on into the deep canyon.

"It's there, Justice. Can you smell it?"

"All I can smell is trouble, Keep. Have you thought of pulling out of here, of coming back with a larger party another time."

"Another time?" The foxy little face turned toward Ruff. "Like when? It's late in the year, Justice. By the time I could get organized again, the snow would be falling. It would be too late. Next spring? Uh-uh. Too much could happen. I could have people from Lode flooding the badlands. No. This is my claim and I'm here to take what I can get. Now!"

With that, Keep swung aboard and rode off, following the silver-gray river up the canyon, followed by Rupert Hallop and the single remaining sheepherder.

"I don't like this," Sarah Farmer said.

"No? I don't either."

"I wanted to find my brother—I still do—but this place . . ." She shook her head.

"Clear the trail there," Horace Cobb called angrily, and they backed their horses to let the professor by. The professor and his woman. Gertrude rode her horse uneasily, gripping the reins tightly in both fists. Her back was rigid, her jaw set.

"There's another one of us wishes she were home," Ruff said.

"Poor Gertrude," Sarah said very softly.

Poor Gertrude, poor Sarah, poor everyone, Justice thought. But that wasn't productive thinking, and so he heeled the black, moving ahead down the river bottom, seeing the red-faced cliffs through the parting clouds, seeing the small, irregular smudges against them, knowing what they were—the openings to those high-up caves.

The rain drove down yet, the clouds drawing shut again, closing out the view of the cliffs and the bluffs above. It was somewhat comforting. If they couldn't see the sniper's position, perhaps he couldn't see them.

They found the old camp a mile on.

There wasn't much to mark it. A stone fire ring, a clutter of rusted tin cans to one side, a lean-to made of willow logs thrown up in a hollow.

"That's it," Keep said, and he was down from his horse, wading into the gravel-bottomed creek. He bent down, scooped up a handful of sand, and held it up to the light, the water trickling down his arm. He glanced at Justice, grinned, and started walking upstream.

"What the hell's he up to?" Duggs muttered. "Has he gone crazy?"

No one answered the corporal. Ruff had gotten down and begun poking around the camp. There wasn't much to find that they hadn't already seen. Back in the hollow behind the lean-to was a collection of tools wrapped in canvas, heavily oiled but rusting nevertheless: picks, shovels, axes, sledgehammers.

Ruff glanced back across his shoulder. Keep was still in midstream, and now his hands were raised to the heavens. The wind shook the willows around the camp. A stray beam of sunlight slashed through the clouds and glinted off the rapidly running river.

Justice frowned. In the hollow with the tools was a pile of firewood covered with tent canvas. Someone had been at the wood. Someone had been in there within the past few days.

Ruff could see clearly the dark impressions where other logs had lain. There were still insects—pincer bugs—moving around in the hollows, insects that would have been gone if the wood had been disturbed some time ago.

No, it was very recent.

"Are we ready?"

Ruff Justice turned toward the voice. Cobb was there, a rope across his shoulder. "Mr. Justice, I say, are we ready?"

"Ready for what, Professor?" Justice asked, strolling that way.

"Professor Eccles and I mean to cross the river and have a climb before dusk."

"To look at the caves, you mean?"

"Yes, of course."

"You're cutting it kind of fine, aren't you? You'd be better off to wait until morning."

"That may be so. However, after traveling all this distance to locate the caves of the Stone Warriors, I don't intend to procrastinate now. Surely you understand that."

"Yes," Ruff answered reluctantly. "I guess I do."

"Since Dr. Eccles is going with me, I thought it best to take you along as a guard. Not that I seriously expect to find aboriginal giants still living in these hills, but there is the chance, isn't there?" His eyes got bright again, as bright and greedy as Keep's. Maybe, Justice thought, the professor was as greedy in his own way. What did it mean professionally to a man like Cobb to make a discovery like this?

"You will climb with us, I assume?" Cobb said with some impatience. "You won't forget that this entire venture is under the auspices of the Department of the Interior specifically for scientific discovery—and not a gold-seeking pilgrimage."

"I won't forget, Professor. Fortunately the gold bug's never gotten a good grip on me. Mr. Keep seems to be seriously affected just now, however."

"That is Keep's business and none of mine," Cobb snapped. Now that he felt he had established the working relationship with Ruff Justice, he was riding high. "Since we will have to return after only a cursory exploration, time being against us, we will take only climbing equipment. In the morning you will have to make packs up for us—food, scientific equipment from our stores . . ."

Ruff nodded as he walked beside the professor. He nodded but had no intention of doing. He was no man's lackey and never would be. Cobb would likely complain to the army—if they ever got back—but the professor couldn't have understood Ruff's special relationship with the military. They needed him as much as, if not more than, he needed them. He took orders, would never desert a force in trouble, but when it came to plain foolishness, Justice drew the line. There was right and there was wrong in his mind; there was also a line between what was acceptable for a gentleman scout and what was not. Making up a pack for some effete scientist and his squaw didn't fall into the acceptable category.

"Kind of late for this nonsense, ain't it?" Hallop asked as Ruff prepared for the climb.

"The professor's all excited about it."

"Is he carrying a gun?" Hallop was crouched against the earth, a cigarette dangling from his lips.

"I doubt it."

"I sure would be." Hallop looked across the swollen gray creek toward the bluffs. "After what I've seen, I sure as hell would be carrying me a gun."

"Are you staying here?" Justice asked.

"You bet your life I am."

"You and Keep and the gold."

Hallop's eyes grew cautious. "That's right."

"You'd better make damn sure you have a gun on in any case, wouldn't you say?"

"What in hell are you trying to tell me, Justice?" Hallop demanded.

"I'm just telling you to be careful—same as you were telling me." Ruff grinned and turned away. He found a worried-looking Alvin Duggs standing beside Sarah Farmer. There was a fire burning now and Ramón the Basque, the last sheepherder, was tending it, looking grave and dark, perhaps wondering what devil had brought him to this foreign land.

"What's the matter?" Ruff asked the corporal.

"Chambers hasn't come in yet. He's overdue."

"It's rough riding country," Justice said, looking to the bluffs where he had sent the cavalryman. "Give him time."

"And if he doesn't come in before dark?"

"Nothing." Ruff leveled a finger at Duggs. "You stay put and stay close to Miss Farmer until I get back." He thought of telling Duggs about his conviction that someone had been at the wood supply in the hollow, but he decided against it.

"I don't like this," Alvin Duggs said soberly. "Not a damned bit, I don't. I've fought Cheyenne and Sioux, I've fought white renegades down on the border, Mr. Justice, but this is different. What are we fighting? Who are they? Where? I've lost my men one by one and I haven't even seen the damned enemy."

"Easy, Corporal."

"Yes, sir." Duggs hung his head a little. The fire was going good now and Ramón had put the coffeepot on to boil.

"Well!" Professor Horace Cobb, a coil of rope over his shoulder, was waiting, hands on hips.

"Let's have at it," Justice said.

"Ruff!" Sarah ran to him in three short, hurried steps and put her arms around his shoulders. Stretching out on tiptoes, she kissed him deeply. "Careful, big man," she whispered.

He squeezed her arm and nodded to the professors Cobb and Eccles, who looked antsy and quite nervous. "Let's go."

They waded the rapidly running creek, Gertrude nearly swept from her feet once. The water wasn't more than two feet deep, but it was moving damned fast and spreading as the rain continued upstream. They crossed a very narrow beach and stood looking up through the misty drizzle toward the red, time-eroded bluffs overhead.

"It seems there was once a trail there, Gertrude," Cobb was saying. "Between the first and second levels. Ladders would have been used to reach the first level."

The woman's head bobbed up and down, but if she were having any significant thoughts, she was holding them for later.

Ruff was holding his thoughts as well, as they were a little more scary than the conjecture about how the primitive cave dwellers had reached their homes. He had seen him—not once, but twice, high on the bluffs. A dark, moving shadow, crouched low. It wasn't Private Chambers, and that meant it wasn't any of their people at all.

"Can we get up there?" Cobb asked.

There had been a landslide some time back, forming a ramp of rubble that, though seeming steep and hazardous, led to the trail the professor had observed.

"We can try it," Ruff said. "I'll go first. Watch for falling rock."

He went onto the rubble and began to climb, his eyes on the bluff a hundred feet above. The rain fell more steadily now, stinging his eyes, shutting out the view of the cliff tops.

Ruff reached the trail fifty feet above the beach and stood there looking down. He waved an arm, and Gertrude Eccles started up, looking awkward and frightened.

The river rushed by down the long gorge, cutting through the badlands toward the distant prairie. Ruff could see the fire of the camp across the stream, like a hazy, distant beacon.

The trail he now stood on was ancient, very ancient, time-scarred, smoothed by numberless feet. He had seen cliffside houses like this in the Southwest, in Arizona and New Mexico. Nowhere else. Where had those Indians learned to build like that, like nothing else seen on the continent?

Cobb was beside him, wheezing and gasping. Mist covered his spectacles. Gertrude Eccles looked ready to faint.

"It's old, very old," Cobb was saying to himself. "They've been here for a long while."

"They may still be here," Ruff cautioned the scientist.

"Yes," Cobb replied, and he was either very brave

or a little mad. "Let's go on, quickly. Quickly before dark. I must have a look."

They inched forward down the narrow broken trail as thunder boomed down the long, rain-washed canyon. Ruff could see the mouth of the cave ahead of him, not more than thirty feet. He jumped the little gap in the trail, heard sand and gravel roll off to the base of the cliff, and then he was there.

In another minute Cobb was beside him with Gertrude, who was nearly ignored by the scientist in his excitement.

"There," Cobb said softly. "Wait a minute. Let's have a torch."

Ruff waited as he lit it. He wasn't anxious to go in himself. He could smell not life but death in the cave. The old musty, indefinable odors of meat that has rotted away, desiccated, turned to dust. The odors of ancient life and of eternal death.

Ruff felt the corner of his mouth draw up tightly. The professor lit a match to start the torch and they proceeded, ducking low to clear the rock overhead.

Inside, the cave opened up rapidly. The smoky torch-light cast moving shadows across the reddish walls of a vast cavern. The floor of the cave was domed, but fairly even; the ceiling high, ragged.

"Look at that," Cobb said in the hushed tones of a pilgrim to a holy city. He moved toward the wall opposite and Ruff walked with him. There was a cave painting there, like a primitive tapestry—painted in blood? "Here, and look there. Gertrude, do you see it?"

A vast herd of buffalo were depicted, and in the foreground several were being skinned and quartered. Hunched over the dead bison were half a dozen men. Every one of them wore a red beard to the middle of his chest.

Ruff felt those icy little fingers crawl up his spine again. Before him the dead lived, prehistory walked and hunted and ate bloody flesh. Cobb was so absorbed that he didn't see Gertrude sway and start to faint. Ruff caught her and held her until she recovered herself and angrily shook away from him.

"Here, Gertrude," Cobb said, moving toward a vast pit against the south face of the cavern. Ruff walked after them, the flaring torch painting long shadows across the floor, up along the curved ceiling. Wavering, moving shadows not quite belonging to Ruff and the scientists. The pit was filled with bones.

Gertrude stood gaping. Cobb was scribbling furiously in a notebook. Ruff took the torch from under the professor's arm and dropped into the shallow pit, working his way across it. The bones were overwhelmingly buffalo, with here and there deer, fox, badger, cougar—and, yes, human bones. Ruff found a femur, a human pelvis, a skull. These were different from the rest—they, and only they, had been smashed to splinters.

Ruff waded back through the bones. Digging underneath, he discovered that the pit was six to ten feet deep, depending on where you stood. The bones at the bottom were time-yellowed, ancient. Ruff dug one up and tossed it to the professor.

"I don't recognize this," the professor said, turning it over. "Wait, yes, I do—musk-ox. Musk-ox! There haven't been any in Dakota for centuries. Look, Gertrude. A musk-ox rib."

Gertrude looked as if she wanted to vomit. Before climbing up, Ruff took a buffalo bone from the top of the pile. He handed the torch to Cobb and then crouched down over the bone.

"What are you doing?" Gertrude asked.

Ruff didn't answer. He took a stone from the floor of the cavern, a stone used many times before by other hands, and shattered the bone with it. Then he tossed the stone to one side. It rang away. He parted the bone and dug into it with the point of his bowie knife.

Cobb knew what he was doing and he hung over Justice, asking hoarsely, "Well?"

Ruff didn't speak. For an answer he lifted the bone to Cobb's inspection. The professor sucked in his breath sharply and whispered some indecipherable expletive.

"What is it?" Gertrude Eccles asked.

"The marrow—it's still fresh," Cobb answered. "This animal was killed, its bones dumped into this pit within the last week. They are here," he said in a whisper. "The Stone Warriors are alive."

# 12

―――•••――◆――•••―――

It seemed like a hell of a good time to get out of there. The torch was burning low, the cave growing darker and colder. Outside, the rain had increased. Ruff could hear the hiss and drum of it, hear the rush of the wind.

The pile of bones at their feet lay like yellowed ackstraws, devil's playthings. The hunting mural on the wall seemed to come to smoky life. Smudged brown buffalo standing motionless before red-bearded giants . . .

"I want to get out of here," Gertrude Eccles said, her voice rising to shrill hysteria.

"For heaven's sake, Gertrude," Cobb said with astonished disapprobation. "We are going soon. I merely want to sketch the mural in case—"

"I want to go now," she shrieked, her voice rising to a banshee wail on the last word.

"Well, of course," Cobb replied, his eyes widening behind steamy bifocals, "though I can't believe we're in any real danger. They wouldn't return to their home if strangers were here. They seem to be shy, very shy to have avoided—"

"Now!"

"Yes." The professor adjusted his bifocals. "Certainly." He looked to Justice for support and understanding, but didn't find it. Ruff wasn't sure the hysterical woman wasn't the one using common sense just then.

"The torch won't last much longer," was all Ruff said.

Cobb glanced toward the mouth of the cave. Already it was growing dark outside.

"I wouldn't want to climb that cliff face in the darkness," Justice said.

"No, of course not, you're both right," Cobb said. He looked around once more with vast regret. Beyond that cavern was another, and beyond it still more. Above them were two more levels of caves, carved out of the red stone by generations of Stone Warriors. "I've waited this long; I suppose I can wait until morning."

They returned to the mouth of the cave and worked their way down the broken trail, the torch hissing in the falling drizzle, splashing red stains on the bluff behind them. The wind was a howling, whispering thing, and on that night it made noises like human voices. The river was cold, rising as they made their way across it in the near-darkness. Gertrude's teeth were chattering. She looked pale and exhausted as they went up to the campfire to dry off.

Sarah rushed up to Ruff and hugged him. It was a nice welcome, but it worried him.

"What's the matter?" he asked.

"Just everything," she said. She wiped back a strand of hair with nervous fingers and then shrugged. "I'll get you some coffee, all right?"

"Fine."

Together they went to the fire. Ramón, dark-eyed shrunken, hunched against the earth, holding a ti cup in both hands. He wore a big knife at his waist that Ruff had never seen before.

"*Buenas noches*, Ramón."

"*Buenas noches*," the man replied unhappily. Ruff left him to his thoughts; he obviously wasn't in the mood for conversation.

"Here." Sarah handed him a steaming cup and Ruff took it, leading her aside. They sat together on a fallen cottonwood, watching the fire, the dark figure beside it.

"Okay, what's up, and where's everyone else?"

"That's just it," Sarah said in a forceful whisper. "Everyone is gone."

"What do you mean gone?"

"Ruff, you know what gone means," she teased. "Corporal Duggs went to find his man, Chambers. Neither of them came back. Keep and Hallop wandered off somewhere, and there you are. Ramón and I sat across the fire trembling for each other. He's a very superstitious man and very frightened. I'm not very superstitious, and I'm twice as frightened."

"Where in hell would Keep go this time of night?"

"He had lanterns with him. And the diary—that damnable diary. Sometimes I wish it had never been found."

Ruff held her with one arm, drinking his coffee with the other. "Has anyone been around?" he asked suddenly.

"What do you mean?" Sarah's head lifted. "Who could be around? Them? The Stone Warriors?"

"No, not them. Just an idea I had. I thought maybe you'd be having company."

"And so you left me alone!" Her expression changed slowly, growing curious, soft. "Who, Ruff? Who did you think might come around?"

Ruff hesitated. He wasn't sure, but the girl had the right to know. He took another drink of his coffee.

"Your brother, Sarah. Andrew Jackson Farmer. I don't think he's dead. I think he's out there somewhere . . ."

"Then, why . . . ?"

Ruff held up a hand. "I don't think he's quite right, Sarah. I think something happened to him."

"To his mind, you mean."

"Maybe."

"You can't know that. You can't know anything about Andy."

"No, but I can make a few good guesses. Someone's been trailing us, Sarah. At first I thought it was Regis Cavanaugh, but I doubt that. Even Cavanaugh wouldn't go in for the sort of indiscriminate sniping we've been subjected to."

"The Stone Warriors, then," she said almost desperately, "or the Sioux."

"We know it's not the Sioux, Sarah. A lone Sioux with a single rifle? As for the Stone Warriors, it's not their way either, is it? Not from what we know of them. No one's ever seen one fire a rifle. No one's ever seen one, as a matter of fact."

"It could be anyone else, for any of a dozen reasons. Someone from out of your past, for instance. Someone with a grudge against Ruff Justice," she said almost eagerly.

"If it is someone after me in particular, he's the worst damn shot I ever ran up against," Ruff said. "No. He's got a rifle and he knows this area. That eliminates almost everyone."

"What do you mean he knows this area?"

"He's managed to stick to the bluffs and keep up with us. We haven't laid eyes on him." He hesitated and then told her, "Whoever he is, Sarah, he knows where this camp is, knew where to find firewood."

"You mean he's been here. Into camp?"

"Within the last day or so."

"No." She buried her face in her hands and shook her head. She was growing convinced, and she didn't want to be convinced. Not now. She didn't want to know that Andy Farmer was alive if he was the one shooting people. If that was Andy's work, it meant that he was plain insane and that someone was going to have to take him down. Ruff Justice.

"I don't understand it," Sarah said. "If . . . if it is Andy, why would he do it? Kill those people, I mean."

"Crazy men don't need a lot of reasons," Ruff answered, "but I'd guess he's trying to protect his claim. Who knows?"

"I don't want it to be him," she said almost desperately. "I don't want anyone else to be killed."

"No one will be, if I can help it," Ruff said, and there was something in his tone that alerted Sarah.

"What do you mean? What do you intend to do?"

"The only thing there is to do. I'm not going to sit here and wait for him to murder me—or you. When it gets full dark, I'm going hunting. I'm going to find the sniper."

"He'll kill you."

"Maybe." Ruff upturned his cup and poured the dregs out onto the damp earth. "But I'm not going to give him any help. This is the last thing he'll expect, Sarah. It's the last thing I would expect. In the darkness and rain, he'll be feeling fairly secure. He won't believe anyone could find him, or be willing to try."

"But can you find him?"

"Oh, yes." Ruff looked to the dark bluffs above the gold camp. "I'll find him, Sarah, believe me. I only hope he's not your brother."

"If it is"—her hands gripped his arm tightly, her fingers digging into his flesh—"you can't kill him. You've got to promise me that you won't kill him."

Ruff didn't answer. It was the one promise he couldn't make her. "I'm hungry." He rose and helped Sarah to her feet. "Let's see what Ramón's got in that stew pot."

While they were eating, Keep and Hallop came in. Both were soaked to their hips, both carried lanterns now extinguished. Hallop looked cool, his dark, scarred face confident and accepting.

Keep looked like he had discovered a lost valley of naked virgins.

"Where have you been?" Sarah asked directly. "Surely not prospecting by lantern light?"

"That's just it, Miss Farmer," Keep said, rubbing his hands together as he crouched down before the fire. "Prospecting by lantern light."

"You may as well tell the lady about it," Ruff Justice said, "seeing that she's your partner."

"Yes, we are partners, aren't we?" Keep seemed to chew on that for a while, perhaps remembering that while he had his brother's share, Sarah Farmer had two—her father's and her brother's.

"I take it you found it," Ruff said.

"Found what?"

"The mother lode, the source, the high-grade stuff."

"Yes, I found it," Keep said. He grinned at Hallop as if needing the other man's reassurance. "A wall of gold—I swear to you, Justice! A wall of gold!"

"A small wall, I take it," Justice said calmly. He was used to prospector's hyperbole. A thread became a vein, which became a river or a wall.

"Sure, laugh about it, you stupid . . . It's there, I'm telling you."

"All right. How in the hell are you going to get it out?" Ruff asked.

"What do you mean? We'll just . . ." He didn't seem to know after all, and Ruff shook his head, spooning up more of Ramón's stew.

"What is the problem?" Sarah wanted to know.

"Equipment," Ruff counted out on his fingers, "labor,

transportation. Gold ore is heavy. It can't be crushed here. That means transporting it to Lode, where they've got an ore crusher. The first time that is done, we'd have a first-class gold rush on. But it won't be done because you've got only one wagon—and not a suitable one for hauling ore. You've got no miners. And you're not going to work it yourself—someone out there with a gun is not going to let you. That's not mentioning the Stone Warriors." Ruff lifted his eyes to look at the deflated Keep. "Do I have to ask where the source of the gold is?"

Gregory Keep only shook his head. Sarah was interested, "Where is it? I don't understand."

"Near or in the bluffs. Near or beneath the Stone Warriors' cave dwellings. Do you wonder that they've been ferocious? The Spanish, the Sioux, the English, or the French—anyone who's come across that wall of gold must have coveted it, and the first thought that comes into a man's mind must be how to get rid of the Stone Warriors."

"How do they . . ."

"By trying to kill 'em off, I'd guess," Ruff answered. "Any outsider must be the enemy to the Stone Warriors. They maybe don't understand the reasons behind it, but they know the outsiders want them eliminated."

"But they're not here, are they?" Keep asked. "Where the hell are they? What are they but a myth? Who's seen one?"

"I've seen their work," Ruff answered softly. The firelight painted eerie shadows on Keep's face. "I've been in their cave tonight. Ask Cobb if they're real or not."

"Yes," Keep said with force, "but where are they now? Last year, thirty years ago, they might have been here—"

"Within the month. I found bones up there with marrow in them still."

"You what?" Keep nearly came to his feet. He and Hallop exchanged an unhappy look. "You're making it up."

"For what purpose?"

"You're working for the girl."

"Think what you want."

"Where could they be?" Sarah asked.

"Hunting, most likely. But they'll be back. They've lived in those caverns for thousands of years. They won't have simply abandoned them now, not for the convenience of a few gold seekers."

Keep had enough to think about for a time and he fell silent, eating quickly before going off to change his pants. Duggs still hadn't returned from looking for his lost trooper. Cobb and Gertrude were at the fire speaking excitedly of a lot of points Ruff couldn't follow. He gestured Sarah aside.

"You're going now?" she asked in the darkness. She held both of his arms, sagging against him so that her pelvis met his, so that her soft full breasts were flattened against his chest.

"Yes, and don't try to charm me out of it," Ruff said lightly, but not lightly enough perhaps. Sarah looked downcast. She pulled away a little.

Ruff lifted her chin with his finger. "Have you got a pistol?"

"Just an old .41 Remington, but—"

"Do you keep it with you?"

"No."

"Do it. Keep it loaded and near at hand."

"Why, Ruff? Who am I frightened of?"

"You're not kidding me, are you? This is a very bad situation, extremely bad. You've got the savages out there somewhere, the sniper, possibly an Indian, possibly a madman, and Gregory Keep."

"Why would Mr. Keep . . . ? Oh!"

"That's right. A wall of gold. One other point—hide

those file claim papers we found. They weren't notarized, you know."

"What do you mean?"

"What I mean is your father hadn't yet established legal claim to the strike. He wouldn't have, you see. He would have stayed here panning what he could, leaving the paperwork until they got back to Lode with their bags full of dust."

"Then the gold isn't mine . . ." She sounded lost as she said it.

"No, not yet anyway. Does it matter?"

"Not in the way you think, but I did count on having something to live on, Ruff. For God's sake, a woman has to live too, doesn't she?"

"Sure. I'm not trying to pick on you, lady. I'm just telling you how it is. Keep would give anything to know that no one has a legal claim on this find. You keep that paper out of sight. And," he reminded her, "keep the .41 within reach."

"Ruff . . ." she started to say something else, but Justice drew her near and smothered her lips with his own, tasting the sweetness of her watery mouth, feeling her body sag against his. And dammit, this wasn't the time or place for what he was thinking.

"Stay near to someone—Ramón or the professors. Maybe they're not much, but they'll keep Gregory Keep from trying anything." He hoped. "If Duggs comes back before me, you can trust him." He hoped.

When it was full dark, Ruff Justice pulled out without saying a word to anyone. The rain continued to drizzle down; the creek was still rising.

It didn't take long for the campfire to be swallowed up by the darkness and the rain. By the time Ruff reached the creek, he was in total darkness. He waded across the stream for the third time that day and started up.

He climbed to the south of the Stone Warriors' caves,

finding and using a trail he had spotted on the firs
climb. The trail led to the bluffs above and beyond th
caves. It was there Ruff had seen the lone man, th
hunter, the one who had to die.

It was dark and cold, the going slow. Ruff's buck
skins were heavy with water. The trail was not a
difficult one, but the conditions made it difficult. Ruf
took it slowly, not wanting to fall back, not wanting t
meet anyone or anything unexpectedly.

He slipped frequently, and he was glad he had electe
to leave the Spencer behind. Thunder hammered a
the night, and the wind thrust against his back. Th
rain was cold now. There was no sound audible abov
the storm.

Glancing below him as he paused for breath, Ruf
could see white where the stream purled and foame
over river-bottom rocks. That was all he could see.

He started climbing again, very cautiously, stayin
as low as possible. Somewhere above him, beyond th
rim, the sniper had made his camp.

Ruff crested the bluff and started circling north
ward through the high manzanita brush, the wind ir
his face, the undergrowth scratching at his legs anc
arms. He moved in a crouch, like some wild, primitiv
thing himself. Just then he was primitive, savage. He
had all the instincts of primitive man; the same blooc
flowed in his veins. His eyes were as sharp, his hear
ing as acute. A man only has to learn to use his
hunter's skills, his wilderness senses, and Ruff hac
learned in hard times, hard places.

He saw the clearing ahead of him and stopped dead
The clouds scudded by, brushing the rim of the bluf
with their cottony skirts. There was something there
Something moving, dark and bulky. Ruff saw it anc
then did not as the clouds cut off his vision. He begar
to circle right, his Colt in his hand, his damp hair ir

his eyes, his heart racing, pushing the blood through his arteries.

What he had seen was very large, large and naked, matted hair hanging down across its shoulders, a long peltlike beard growing to midchest.

Unless Ruff was beginning to imagine things too. It was a night for such imaginings: cold, windy, thundering. The clouds twisted past like spun cotton, obscuring all, then suddenly clearing to give a glimpse of the badlands, black and convoluted, running away to the distances.

The Stone Warrior came up out of the ground with a roar, and the massive club it carried thudded off Ruff's shoulder as his Colt stabbed flame once and then was knocked free to clatter away on the rock underfoot. Ruff was falling and he threw his arms up to try to block the ferocious blows of the Stone Warrior's club, but it was no good. The thing was gigantic, wild as any grizzly, brutal and pagan—and it had come to kill.

# 13

Lightning flashed and Ruff Justice went down hard on his back. Jumbled images collided in his mind as he groped for comprehension, as he lashed out savagely with knee and fist, forearm and skull, trying to beat back the mauling thing that had him in its grasp.

By the lightning burst Ruff had seen it clearly, for a split second in time. Huge, bare-chested, red-bearded. There were blue and red beads in its shaggy hair, a beaded chest covering of some sort beneath the beard. There were tattoos on its face and arms. Its eyes were stark cold blue, as blue as Ruff's own. The nose was bridged and wide, the arms massive. The broad mouth had been open, showing broken teeth.

Ruff Justice saw that in a brief, urgent moment. Then his back hit and the Stone Warrior landed on top of him, the club rising.

The Colt had spoken once, missed, and been clubbed away. Now Justice had only his bare hands against this monster—and how many others? Were there others that would come running to help savage him, to tear his joints apart and crush his bones?

That thought gave Justice the strength of desperation.

134

He wriggled frantically, trying to kick aside the Stone Warrior. The club that had already struck tellingly arced down again, and Ruff managed to block it with crossed forearms that caught the Stone Warrior at the wrist. Still the club came down and rang off his skull, but not with the bone-crushing power the Stone Warrior had intended.

Ruff gripped the warrior by the beard and yanked his head down, slamming his skull into the thing's face. The nose broke and Ruff felt hot blood spray his face as the Stone Warrior threw back his head and howled at the dark and tumbling skies.

Ruff tried to follow up with a forearm thrown at the Stone Warrior's throat, but the thing backed away, striking at Ruff now with fists, aiming at the groin, the belly.

Justice was strong, skilled, but the man on top of him was like no man—red, black, or white—he had ever tangled with. The fists were like the hooves of a horse thudding down, the weight and strength behind them incredible, the pain numbing as they landed.

Ruff rolled aside to protect his groin, kicked back with his boot and caught flesh, pawed at his bowie, and came to his feet.

Lightning flickered again, distantly, and Ruff saw the Stone Warrior's face for the second time. It was a foot above Ruff's own head, a bloody, savagely unintelligent face without emotion or apparent fear. War was life, life was war. The Stone Warrior waited until the lightning died and then launched himself at Ruff Justice.

Ruff stepped back, tried to trip the savage, simultaneously struck down with his clenched hand at the back of the Stone Warrior's neck, and felt a pawing hand grip his shirt front and slide away. Ruff kicked out blindly, feeling his boot toe meet muscle and bone, sinew and hide, living muscle that had the quickness, the resiliency of a cougar.

The thing had been down and now it was up again. Ruff had clubbed it with all of his strength, and it hadn't done a damn thing to slow it down. The enemy was huge, but more than that, his body had been exerted to the extreme every living day. Life was a struggle against the elements, the multitude of enemies. Each day meant climbing hills, running down game, fighting those who would crush you. It had the strength of the barbarian—incredible power, vast reserves developed from years of warring with life itself.

The Stone Warrior bawled and came in again, and Ruff cut up with his bowie. Steel found flesh and the thing roared with fury, rearing back, slapping at the knife with both hands. It feinted and then moved in again, but it wasn't quick enough for Ruff, who cut to his right, taking a finger or two from the Stone Warrior's hand.

He was bitten, but he wasn't going to let this strange creature get the best of him. The thing came in again, its head low, hands hanging, low mewling sounds coming from its lips.

Justice was cautious, but confident. He had done some knifework in his time and the thing before him was unarmed.

"Just take off, friend," Ruff said soothingly, much as he might have talked to a stalking panther. "Take off and live—I've got no quarrel with you."

It didn't understand the words and didn't comprehend the sentiment. In the Stone Warrior's world there was no such concept. To retreat was to cease to be a warrior. To run away was worse than dying, much worse. Then you had lived for nothing. A coward was not a man, a beast, an angel, a spirit, it was nothing at all—a coward did not exist.

Ruff sensed all of this without knowing how or why. He sensed it because he was that kind of man himself. How long did a coward last on the plains, in the mountains? What use was a man who wasn't worth his word, who wouldn't side with you when the chips were down? Ruff knew the thing before him and he could respect it.

"I wish you'd take off, though, damn you," he said in a low voice.

They had worked their way nearer to the edge of the bluff. The wind shrieked through the convolutions in the time-eroded cliffs. Far below, the river rampaged, growing higher, wider with each hour.

The Stone Warrior still came in, Ruff backing, circling, the knife held low, not wanting to kill the thing, knowing that he would have to.

The little icy fingers were there again. Ruff felt his body tense, ready itself before he had even identified the danger. When he did identify it, it was already too late.

Behind him he heard one small, muffled sound. A bare foot on wet stone and there was time to start a turn, to deepen the crouch before the second Stone Warrior was on top of Ruff Justice, a cry of triumph rising from its throat.

The rifle exploded in the night. Blinding red-white light stabbed across the bluff and the Stone Warrior bellowed with pain. Ruff felt the body collide with his own, saw the second Stone Warrior turn, slip, and then topple over the edge of the bluff to cartwheel through space toward the river below; its animal scream filling the night before a peal of thunder overpowered the bloodcurdling sound.

Justice had been knocked flat again, and this time his head had rung off the stone beneath him. There was something on top of him, something heavy, smell-

ing of dead meat, like a buffalo skinner's coat, and
Justice couldn't figure what it was. His head sparked
and spun, drifted away on a length of elastic, snap
ping back suddenly, jolting the delicate little brain
that floated inside the case of bone.

*Stone Warriors.*

Justice tried to come to his feet, tried to strike out
with the knife. The fall had knocked the balance out
of him, and he toppled over, feeling the wind rush
past, the rain against his flushed cheek.

"Come on, you." The hand reached out and took
Ruff's.

Justice started to fight back, then stopped. Whoever
that was, he wasn't an enemy or Justice would have
already been dead. The figure standing over him had
a rifle in his hand—the rifle that had saved him from
the second Stone Warrior moments earlier, and Jus
tice let himself be helped to his feet.

"Let's get out of here. There's more around. Plenty
of them," the stranger said.

"Listen . . ."

"Quiet. Let's go now, talk later. Here."

Ruff felt something cool and solid pressed into his
hand. Even with the fog of confusion, the swirling of
his senses, he recognized it for the butt of his Colt,
and he took it.

"Follow me. Silently, please."

The man moved off and Ruff started after him.
Thunder boomed again, sounding like a chorus of an
gry voices, and the wind increased. His guide dipped
down into a brushy hollow, followed a narrow stream
that ran through a stony V cut in the bluff by aeons of
similar freshets, climbed a crumbling denuded cliff
and finally halted, gasping for breath. Ruff squatted
beside him, staring out at the night, down the back
trail, his head slowly clearing.

"Andy Famer?" Justice asked.

"That's right."

They crouched side by side in the darkness and rain, watching silently for half an hour. "We've lost them," Farmer said at last. "Come on now—my fortress isn't far from here."

Ruff's thinking did a few quick switches. He had come out hunting Andrew Jackson Farmer, meaning to have his head. To his mind Farmer was a sniper-killer, half-mad, dangerous as hell. Now Andy had saved his bacon.

The rain fell harder. Before them somewhere were the Stone Warriors. There was no way out that Ruff knew but to tag along with Farmer.

"Let's go."

Farmer led off through the night, the underbrush close and tangled. Overhead the sky was blotted out, and Ruff could smell the sharp tang of cedar.

Farmer dipped into a hollow, turned right to follow a shallow watercourse that ran through a stony chute—the upper end of the gully Ruff had crossed earlier, he guessed. Then they clambered through a stack of boulders, following a weaving course toward the crest of the bluff, which was set back from the cliff face, the highest point of visible land for miles around.

"This way." Andy was climbing again. Up ten feet, along a narrow lip of ledge, and into a warm, small cavern that smelled of wood smoke.

"This is home?" Ruff said, looking around.

"This is it." Andy grinned in the darkness.

Ruff nodded appreciatively. The enemy would have a tough time slipping through that tangle of brush silently, a tougher time climbing the rocks without alerting anyone above.

"Do they know where you are?" Ruff asked.

"No. That is, I don't think so." Andy was crouched over a small hollow in the stone floor of the cavern. Flint sparked and he bent lower yet, puffing gently on his tinder until he had a cupful of fire. He turned to face Ruff, adding sticks of fuel at the same time. "They haven't tried to root me out yet. They don't like this gun. They know it speaks pain. What they don't know is how low on ammunition I am."

Ruff didn't say anything. He was studying the man by the wavering firelight, wondering what sort of madman he was seeing. Was he the sniper or just a kid who'd had the rug yanked from under him?

Andy was blond-haired, dark-eyed. His hair had gotten long, curling around his ears and shirt collar. There was a wisp of dark beard on his face. His clothes were rags—out at the elbows and knees, stained, and buttonless.

"You know your sister's here?" Ruff said.

"Sarah!" He took a step toward Ruff. He shook his head; his mouth was literally hanging open. "Why would she be here—doesn't she know about *them*?"

"She knows."

"Does she know they killed my father?" Andy shook his head. He walked back and forth before the fire, his rifle in his hands.

Ruff noticed his boots now, split out the sides, dried and cracked. The kid was growing up hard. If he survived, he would be tough as leather, hard as iron. Some had survived such an upbringing; others cracked. Ruff thought he saw the beginnings of a few fissures.

"You have anything to eat?" Justice asked.

"Jerked venison. Over there." The kid nodded toward a little smoking rack that had been pushed to one side. Ruff took his skinning knife from his boot and helped himself to a slab of smoked meat. Andy was distracted, worried, his eyes fire-bright.

"Why did she have to come out here?"

"Looking for you, for your father," Ruff said.

"She found Dad," Farmer said, and Ruff wasn't sure if Andy knew that because he had been at the funeral, sniping, or not. He seemed at once innocent and guileful, like some young wild thing—cute, cuddly, all teeth and nails.

"Yeah. She found him. Sit down and eat with me," Ruff suggested, thinking he'd like to see that rifle out of the kid's hands for a while.

"No. There's plenty of time to eat later."

"Later?"

"Where is she?" Andy asked, taking off down a fresh trail. "Down in the old camp?"

"That's right. Are you going down with me to see her?"

"I don't think so. Not now . . . Why are they at the old camp? That's my camp, mine and Dad's."

"Everyone figured you were dead. Tom Keep's brother came out here and your sister came with him."

"The gold."

"That's right."

The kid shook his head heavily. "He can't have that gold. It's mine. Dad told me to watch the claim."

"He's Tom Keep's heir."

"That's of no matter. It's my claim. If I see him, I'll . . ." The kid shrugged and grinned.

Ruff wasn't buying the grin. "Why don't you tell me what's happened, Andy."

"You seem to know all of it."

"Not all of it. What's keeping you here?"

"What's keeping me?" Genuine, deep astonishment was reflected on his young face. He came nearer to Ruff, the fire at his back dancing weirdly across the cavern interior. "What do you think is keeping me here?"

"I don't know, Andy. The gold?"

"The gold!" The kid laughed out loud, throwing back his head. The roar of laughter echoed through the cavern hideout. He stopped abruptly and looked soberly at Justice. "I thought you were the kind of man who'd understand me, but I guess I was wrong."

"How could you know what kind of man I am?" Ruff asked casually. He chewed slowly on the jerked meat.

"Maybe I've been watching you. Maybe I've seen how you handle yourself."

"Have you?"

"For gold," Andy said, galloping down another fresh trail. He had a habit of doing that, and it didn't give Ruff a lot of faith in his mind. "I've got enough to keep a man for years. Years!"

"Have you?"

"Sure, me and Dad hid ours when we pulled out."

"But it wasn't enough."

"Enough for us, sure. It was Tom Keep who wanted to stay one more day, one more day, and then they came back."

"The Stone Warriors."

"And now you're saying it." The kid winked and took another step nearer. Now he was within a yard of Ruff, standing over him, his rifle held casually to one side. It would only take a swing of the barrel, a little pressure with the index finger . . .

"Now I'm saying what?" Ruff shook his head, wiped the skinning knife on the leg of his buckskins, and stood up. "I don't follow you, Andy."

"No—you're the one that asked."

"Asked? Why you didn't pull off, you mean?"

"That's right."

"It's because of the Stone Warriors."

"That's it, my friend," the kid answered. "I have to stay. You can see that. I have to stay and kill them. I have to keep killing them, for Dad. If I don't kill them, what kind of man am I?" Andy's voice was rising, wavering. His eyes were far too bright. "But you can't kill them all. That's the joke of it." He sobbed a little, way back in his throat. "Whatever you do, they keep coming. The same twelve of them . . . the same goddamned twelve."

"What are you talking about, Andy?" The kid had lost it now. His shoulders were hunched and he was sobbing freely. He was just a strapping big kid who had taken on something that was too big for him to handle.

"So . . ." He wiped his sleeve angrily across his nose. "I stay and I kill them. I follow them when they hunt. I shoot them from cover and I run away before they can catch me and do me with those clubs they carry." He went on for quite a while, describing each kill. The details were gory, unnecessary. It was almost as if the kid were imagining it, but Ruff didn't think he was.

The whole thing had an air of unreality. Farmer told him, "You kill them but they're not dead. What's the point in it? You kill the same one over and over. You can put out his dead eyes, cut off his fingers, rip open his belly and strew his guts across the earth, trample on them, spit on them, set fire to him. You'll meet him again the next day, the next week—not dead. Not dead at all."

Ruff looked away. He was in the presence of madness and he had never liked that feeling. A man without control of his mind was a terrifying thing. A thoughtless body of muscle and purpose moving across the earth destroying without knowing why.

"What the hell's that?"

Farmer came suddenly alert, his head stretching out on his neck like a wild animal's. Ruff heard it too and he turned toward the cavern mouth. A terrible sound drifted toward them through the night storm. Animal, guttural, primitive.

"Stone Warriors." Andy started toward the mouth of the cave. "They're down there. In the camp. Sarah!"

Andy started off at a run, Justice at his heels. He had taken three strides when the Stone Warriors appeared before them, huge, menacing, deadly.

# 14

There were two of them, wild, savage, bloody. Ruff saw the hand with the severed fingers, saw the wounded abdomen, and he knew—knew this was the Stone Warrior he had fought earlier, had seen fall over the cliff. The Stone Warrior threw back his head and bellowed, charging Justice.

He didn't have a chance. It was light in the cave, the fire behind Ruff burning brightly. Justice drew his Colt easily and fired three times. The first .44 bullet spun the Stone Warrior half around. The second tore his throat out, and the Stone Warrior, gripping his neck with both hands went to the ground, the third bullet already striking home, punching through heart and lungs, finishing the job.

Farmer had taken his man too. The Winchester he carried barked twice, four times, and the Stone Warrior was blown back, writhing and twitching, his massive body filmed with blood, the eyes going empty as Farmer, walking in, fired again, directly into the head this time. The brain and skull exploded across the cavern, destroying anything that might have been recognizably human.

But Farmer wasn't through.

With a shout of triumph the kid leapt forward, and Justice could only watch as Andy Farmer jammed the butt of his rifle into the shattered face of the Stone Warrior, driving it down again and again, pulping flesh and bone.

Ruff grabbed him by the arm and Andy shook him off.

"You've got to smash every bone. Every single bone. Can't you understand that, Justice?"

"They may have your sister, Andy."

"Yes." Farmer looked at the dead thing lying on the floor of the cavern and then back to Ruff Justice. "They might have her. We'd better find out."

They moved out into the night then, the wind a snapping, lashing thing hurling rain against their bodies.

They half-ran, half-slid down the jumble of rocks before the cave. Directly below them but inaccessible from their position was the cliff face that sheltered the three-tiered Stone Warrior cave dwelling. They veered left and started down the stony chute where black water raced. Ruff went down, barked a knee, rose, and raced on, Andy Farmer puffing and moaning ahead of him as he ran. Justice was in the tracks of a madman and at that moment the madman was his only ally against a tribe of Stone Age killers.

Down the long bluff, with lightning striking fire against a cold sky, they reached the river. Andy Farmer, showing the instincts of a hunter, slowed and stilled his breath, crouching to look, to sniff the night air. Ruff was beside him, every fiber of his body stretched taut, alert. They were there somewhere, the Stone Warriors, and they probably had Sarah.

Ruff tapped Andy's shoulder and gestured. Together they waded the black river, feeling the icy current rippling against their bodies. Then they were out of the water and into the wind-battered willows again. The rain was coming in cold gusts. There was no sign of a campfire.

Ruff held back at the edge of the camp, peering across the clearing. The willows around them shuddered in the wind. Andy tapped Ruff's shoulder and jabbed a finger toward the tent Sarah had been sleeping in. Ruff saw it too, a dark, inert form against the ground, the limbs twisted and formless, smashed into unrecognizable shapes.

Andy had learned a lot in his months in the wilderness. He wasn't fool enough to cross the clearing openly, although he was aching to find out. Ruff wanted to know, too. Somehow he didn't think it was Sarah, though he couldn't have said what convinced him it was not.

Andy had begun circling west and south, following the perimeter of the campground. Ruff halted, seeing a shape he did not like, hearing motion, but it was only a young oak in the wind.

Andy halted and whispered into Ruff's ear. "It's not her. A man's clothes." There was an implied question in that statement.

Ruff peered at the dead man, recognizing the checked shirt, the boots. "A man named Ramón. A Spaniard."

Andy nodded, crouching in his tracks to look at Ruff with quickly shuttling eyes. "They've got her," he said.

"I know it."

"They'll use her and then throw her away . . ."

Again Ruff agreed with Andy Farmer. They would use the woman, use her time and again until she broke down and wasn't worth the using. Ruff's eyes followed Andy's to the cliff houses across the dark, rolling river. It was impossible.

"We haven't got a chance in hell."

"Neither has she, if we leave her."

And where in hell were Keep and Hallop? Dead, in pursuit—or on the run out of the country as fast as their horses could carry them? And how about Gertrude and the professor?

"We going?" Andy asked, and even in the darkness Ruff could see the kid's eyes glitter. Was it madness there, or was he plain angry?

"We're going," Ruff said softly. "Damn us, we're going." First he wanted to look through the supplies they had left behind. The Spencer loomed large in Ruff's thinking—he would feel a lot cozier about this with the big gun in his hands.

The .56 wasn't where he had left it. There wasn't a lot of anything left. The Stone Warriors had torn open bags of cornmeal, flour, sugar, coffee, decided that it was all good to eat and taken off with all they could carry. That and knives, blankets, pots and pans . . . and the horses. Damn them, they had the horses, and without them there wasn't a real good chance of ever getting out of this country alive.

"Is that what I think it is?" Andy Farmer asked. Ruff saw him digging in the opened crate. What he had was some of Keep's dynamite and a length of fuse.

"Leave that here," Ruff said.

"The hell with you. I just might find a use for this."

"Sure—blowing us all up."

"You want to stand here and argue about it, Justice?"

"No." The rain slanted down between them. "No, don't. Let's get going. I hope you've got an idea how to go about it."

"Sure. Nothing to it," Andy said, and his confidence worried Justice. It wasn't normal. "We'll go in the back door."

"There's a back way into the cavern?"

"What did I say?" Andy asked lightly.

"Quit telling me and show me. Dammit, Andy, this

isn't a joke. They've got Sarah and they can't have her, you hear me. Let's move it."

"Sure." Andy tucked the dynamite into his shirt and nodded. Again they waded the river and again they climbed the bluffs. There was no sign of life in the darkness. No whisper of sound, no fire, no footfall. Ruff wasn't looking for him and he stepped on him before he saw the man.

"Hold up," Ruff hissed. He saw Andy halt, tense, and start back. He crouched down in the rain beside Justice.

"What is it?"

"What it is, is a Professor Cobb," Justice said.

"Alive?"

"He's alive. He's got a hen's egg on the side of his head." Outside of that, Cobb seemed to be all right. He had lost his spectacles and the coat he wore was missing most of its sleeve, but he seemed to be in one piece.

"Let's go, Justice. Dammit, we can't waste time."

"We can't leave Cobb here."

"No? Why not? What good's he going to be to us, to Sarah, to anybody?"

"He might be able to tell us where they have her, if she's alive."

"She's alive," Andy said. "And I'm going after her. You stay here and nursemaid that dude if you want to. I'm going killing."

"You hate them, don't you? You really hate them?"

"I'll kill every one of them."

"Sarah doesn't matter to you, does she? It's just the killing you want to do."

"Shut up. What are you doing? Leave him here."

Ruff stood, shouldering Cobb. "I'll carry him to your cave. That's where we're going, isn't it?"

"Yeah," Andy said slowly, "that's where we're going."

He turned sharply and started jogging upslope over the dark, broken ground, which he knew like the back of his hand. He went as rapidly as he could, deliberately trying to leave Justice behind.

Ruff stuck with him and they mounted the high bluff nearly together. Ruff's legs were knotted, however, his lungs filled with broken glass. It had been a while since he had done any serious climbing. They halted at the cavern's mouth.

"Where's your bed?" Ruff asked as they went back into the cave.

"Hold it," Andy stopped, holding perfectly still. "Damn—they came and got the dead."

He was right. The Stone Warriors they had killed in the earlier scuffle had gone.

"Sure, they came and got the dead," Andy repeated. But that wasn't what he was thinking. He was thinking that they couldn't be killed. Smashed skulls, broken bones, gouged eyes—none of it mattered. They pulled themselves together and rose again like things coming up out of the grave.

"Where's your bed?" Justice repeated.

"This way."

It was as black as sin in the cave, and Andy inched ahead, taking Ruff's arm to guide him. They had gone twenty feet or so when the kid stopped.

"Hold it here. We've got to have light, like it or not." Ruff saw Andy crouch, saw flint spark, and the battered kerosene lantern came to life.

He had had it in a cleft in the cave wall, hidden carefully away. Now by the lantern light Ruff could see that Andy had been here for some time, planned on being here for more. He had made a bed of grass and old blankets, found a flat slab of rock to use for a table. The lantern flickered and sketched long shadows across the uneven cavern ceiling.

"Put him down and let's get going."

Ruff laid Cobb down. The professor was going to have a few bad moments when he woke up. Alone in the dark, unfamiliar cave he was going to have to just sit tight. It couldn't be helped.

Andy was already moving off and Justice took a dozen quick steps to catch up. They moved down a long funnel-shaped corridor, the light from the lantern illuminating the weird grin on Andy Farmer's face. It seemed to be locked into position. Wholly unnatural, it gave Ruff no feeling of confidence.

"You know where you're going?"

"Don't worry about that."

Their shadows twisted and bent, then disappeared as the trail dropped off sharply. Andy didn't even hesitate. He jumped down six feet to a lower level and proceeded along a ledge that overhung a deeper cavern. Each small sound echoed and reechoed. Ruff had the sensation of vast depths below and he didn't like it much. It brought back old memories.

The ledge ended and Andy unerringly found and climbed a short stony ramp, Justice at his heels.

The kid stopped abruptly. "Hear that?"

Ruff didn't at first. Then he did—a distant soughing sound like wind creaking in the trees. That was what it sounded like at first, but if you listened hard, you could hear the fear, the pain in the unseen voice.

"Move it," Ruff said angrily, but Andy didn't need any encouragement. They trotted ahead down a long corridor carved by water aeons ago as it sought a way out of the heart of the ancient bluff.

The Stone Warrior appeared before them and Ruff shot him full in the face, the pistol shot like thunder shaking the world, rattling in the ears. The Stone Warrior was blasted back to lie writhing, crimped against the floor of the cave, his skull blown around the corridor.

"That's it," Andy said. "No sense being quiet now."

They ran on. They were definitely on a different level now. The rock had changed from sandstone to limestone with flinty outcroppings. They saw bones on the floor now, bunches of grass collected for an uncertain purpose, a broken Sioux lance thrown aside.

And on the walls the great, magnificent paintings, the incredible pictures—primitive, skillful, unreal. Long boats with curved prows and striped sails and on their decks red-bearded soldiers carrying shields and swords.

The gun exploded in Andy Farmer's hands. The Stone Warrior didn't stop running, although the .44-40 had split his brisket open. He had a club upraised, his wildly matted red hair stuck out from his skull in all directions. Blood and purple entrails showed beneath his pale hide. Andy shot him again and then again, slamming him back, and the grin that Ruff had seen earlier was still there, making Andy's face as horrible as that of any Stone Warrior.

But then Andy himself had become a cave dweller, a savage thing, a sort of Stone Warrior. Ruff had the unreal feeling that he was participating in a war for survival that fitted other times, other worlds more than this one.

Only the guns reminded him that it was 1878—guns that spoke and spoke again as the Stone Warriors came shrieking and bellowing from out of the stone alcoves, hurling rocks and clubs. Justice fired from the hip before going to a knee, two-handing the Colt and firing again and again as Andy frantically reloaded.

Ruff's Colt went dry before Andy could make it. Ruff unsheathed the bowie and braced himself, giving a taste of cold steel to the first Stone Warrior. He plunged it into the savage's throat, felt hot blood fountain over his hand and down his arm, felt the writhing of the powerful body in his grasp, the clawing, gouging, clutching hands of the Stone Warrior, which closed around Ruff's throat before the life had run out of the thing.

It stunk of dead hides and raw meat and diseased teeth, and Justice kicked free, jerking his bowie out to crouch and face the next Stone Warrior. The rifle spoke beside his ear and the man went down as Andy Farmer's Winchester stopped the heart of another Stone Warrior.

Then they were gone. Gone but for the dead. The lantern lay on its side against the stone floor of the cavern, leaking kerosene.

They started on, Ruff reloading from his belt loops as they ran. It was two dozen running paces to the elbow in the corridor, a right turn, and they entered the vast cavern chamber beyond.

Gertrude Eccles was on the ground, her skirt above her waist, her blouse ripped off to reveal pink-budded ivory breasts. There was blood on her face and a large spreading bruise. Her eyes were empty of intelligence, her mouth hanging open like an idiot's waggled and trembled, trying to form a word as Ruff reached her.

"Where's Sarah?" Ruff demanded sharply. A Stone Warrior had appeared from out of a feeder tunnel and Andy Farmer shot him, the pealing echoes rolling through the vast cathedrallike cavern.

"They hurt me . . . they touched me . . ." Gertrude was gripping Ruff's arm, gripping it tightly. Her mouth had suddenly remembered how to make sounds and she was making the best of it. "We were sleeping and they came into the camp. I couldn't do a thing. Horace ran—he ran away. They came . . . and started grabbing me. God!"

She buried her face in her hands and Justice bellowed, "Where's Sarah Farmer?"

"Over there. They had her over there." A hand

waved weakly toward "over there," which was a small alcove off the main cavern to Ruff's right. He jerked Gertrude Eccles to her feet and led her, stumbling, that way. Andy backed up, firing his rifle until it was empty, then turning to hotfoot it after them.

She was all right. They found her sitting on the floor of the dark alcove, her legs crossed tailor-fashion, her dress torn, face scratched. Otherwise, she was all right.

"Ruff!"

She tried to get up, and sagged back. Ruff gripped her wrist and brought her to her feet. She caught sight of Andy, who was struggling to jam a fistful of loose cartridges into the magazine of his rifle. A little shriek escaped her lips.

"Andy? Is it you?" She walked toward him and for a moment that mad grin fell away.

"Hello," he said. "They're out there, Ruff. Lots of them. Let's get our tails moving."

It was a damn fine idea. They started back toward the passageway that led up to Andy's cave dwelling. The fuel in the lantern was growing rapidly low. A lot had been spilled out and it worried Ruff—all they needed was to be caught in the darkness with these bastards all around them. Gertrude wasn't up to it. She was barely walking. Ruff figured he would be carrying her soon. The ammunition was low and they weren't gaining a lot of ground on the pursuit.

Even if they did make it to Andy's cave, safety was miles away. Miles across wasteland with two women, no horses, and a batch of blood-lusting Stone Warriors behind them. It didn't look good, it just didn't look good at all. A minute later it looked a hell of a lot worse.

The lantern had been fizzling, fussing, trying to burn but not making it as the fuel was depleted. Now it went out, flat out, and they stood in the darkness pressed together, Gertrude clinging to Ruff's arm while Sarah, exhausted, panting, held on to his hand.

And behind them they could hear the sounds. Slow, shuffling, moaning, softly howling sounds as the Stone Warriors came on, doing as they always had, running their prey to ground.

# 15

Ruff stood in the thick darkness, hearing water drip somewhere, feeling a cold breath of air toy with the back of his perspiration-soaked neck. He was trying to picture the layout of the cavern in his mind and not having much luck at it. They had to trust to Andy's skills—which would have been all right, but the kid was crazy, just plain crazy.

"Ruff . . ." Sarah started to speak, but Ruff shook his arm with irritation, silencing her as they listened. Waited and listened.

Ruff seemed to smell the thing first, as that rotten-meat smell he was growing too accustomed to assailed his nostrils. Nearly simultaneous was the whispered rush of feet, and Justice fired.

The discharge of the Colt painted the cavern in a brief orange-yellow brightness. The face of the Stone Warrior hovering over them was ghastly, crimson and orange. Gertrude screamed and the warrior toppled back over the edge of the trail and into the darkness below, its bellowing cry filling the cavern as darkness returned abruptly, leaving only the glare of that twisted, dying face imprinted on the retina.

"Come on," Andy said sharply. "Lady, take hold of my shirttail and don't let go," he said to Gertrude. "Then you, Sarah. Ruff, try to keep them off us."

They moved slowly off, up the ledge toward the ramp they had used to descend into the cavern. It seemed miles farther than Ruff recalled. He was at the tail end of the party, which crept along a few feet at a time. He held Sarah's petticoat in his left hand, inching forward as Andy tried to find the trail in the near-total darkness.

"No . . ." Gertrude screamed, and Ruff lunged forward, finding her by chance as she fell. Her feet had misstepped and she had gone over the side. If Ruff remembered correctly, it was a good hundred feet down there. He got her by the wrist and dragged her up. She stood sobbing, shaking wretchedly, and he had to slap her face to get her quieted.

"All right?" Andy panted. "Is it all right?" His voice floated out of the darkness, and from out of the darkness Ruff Justice answered, "Let's keep it moving. She'll do."

"It's uphill here. Sarah? It's uphill. Pretty steep. Stay to the left, all right?"

"Yes," Sarah said. She panted the word, not from weariness, but from nervous exhaustion. Ruff felt her hand rest on his in the darkness, then she pulled away and was gone. Ruff followed, leading Gertrude Eccles, who followed him helplessly, going in which ever direction Ruff steered her.

Behind them they still heard the sounds, the muttering, watery sounds of many animals moaning and milling. The next hour was one of the longest in Ruff's life, climbing through the darkness with a madman, two females, one of them hysterical and injured, the Stone Warriors back there, coming—somehow you knew they were coming without being able to see them. They were there; they would come.

"Light!" Andy Farmer hissed it and stopped abruptly. They were once more on their feet, moving along the crescent-shaped ledge. Ruff's eyes picked it out now too—not far above them, but feeble as if the light were coming around an elbow bend in the cavern.

"Where are we?" Ruff asked.

"That should be my cave—or near to it."

"Is it them?" Gertrude's voice rose in a shriek.

"No," Ruff answered soothingly. "Not them." But it might have been. There was no telling. There was nothing to do but go on and find out, because whether the Stone Warriors were ahead of them or not, they were surely behind.

Ruff moved past the women on the narrow trail. There was enough light bleeding into the corridor now to allow them to see shadow and form. Ruff glanced at Andy Farmer and nodded, and together the two men moved into Andy's cave, their weapons cocked and leveled.

The man jumped away from them, his hands going overhead.

"Cobb!"

"Who else would it be? How did I come to be here? Good God, Gertrude, your breasts are bared!" The little man blinked at the woman as if assuring himself he saw what he thought he saw. He had a pair of spectacles on now; he must have had a spare pair concealed on his person.

"You left me," Gertrude Eccles said with awe. She moved nearer to the scientist, unconcerned about her own appearance now. "You ran and left me, Horace."

"Be sensible. What else was there to do? It was a mad scramble for survival. The confusion was vast."

"You just left me," she repeated, shaking her head tiredly.

Ruff Justice had taken one of Andy's old blankets and slit it in the middle, forming a crude poncho for

Gertrude Eccles. He slipped it over her head now and she nodded, not really paying attention. Her eyes were fixed on Horace Cobb. Several illusions had apparently just been shattered.

"Ruff," Sarah said urgently, "we can't stay here, can we?"

"No. Let's move it, Andy."

"Go on. I'm not through with it yet," the kid said. The grin was back on his face.

"What are you talking about? Let's get."

"No."

"Andy?" Sarah looked at him pleadingly, her head cocked to one side.

"Not yet. Get on out of here—Justice knows the way. I'll catch up."

"What are you going to do?" Sarah wanted to know.

"Finish it," Andy Farmer said, and he unbuttoned his shirt partially, revealing the dynamite he still carried.

"I don't . . ." Sarah began, but Horace Cobb, screaming, interrupted her. "No! No, I won't allow it."

"Sit down, Professor, and shut up," Andy said sharply. But Cobb wouldn't be silenced. He moved forward, making a grab for Andy Farmer's arm. Andy casually backhanded him and the professor sat down hard.

"It's not worth it, Andy," Ruff said quietly.

"It is to me."

"You'll go up as well."

"Maybe so, maybe not—but they're going up, all right. Every single one of them! Dead at last. I'm blowing this mountain up and they're going with it to their bloody hell."

"Think, man." Cobb was nearly sobbing. "This is one of the greatest scientific finds of the century."

"To hell with science and to hell with you," Andy said very quietly. "They're filth. Cutthroats, bloody cutthroats. Ruff, you're not going to try and stop me, are you?"

"No, Andy, I'm not going to try to stop you."

"Then get them out of here. I'll catch up if I can. Just get the hell off the bluff because it's going to go. It'll give way like a rotten tree, won't it, Mister Professor? It'll just cave in because the mountain is rotten at its core, isn't that so?"

Cobb didn't respond to the question. "You just don't understand," he was saying as he shook his head. "This is a missing page in history. We have something here that can open new doors. They belong to science, not to a madman with a bundle of dynamite."

Maybe, Ruff was thinking, but it had been his experience that the world always belonged to the boys with the dynamite. There wasn't time for a philosophical discussion.

"Let's go," he said to Sarah, and she nodded, looking worriedly at Andy, knowing she couldn't say anything to change his mind. "Professor?"

"No!"

He tried it again. He leapt forward, and Andy Farmer coldcocked him with the barrel of the Winchester. Cobb went down and no one stepped forward to help him until Justice grabbed his wrists, shouldered him, and with a grunt said to the women, "Now, ladies. So long, Andy. We'll wait at the Little Mo."

"Yes." The kid was concentrating on his fuse; nothing else seemed to hold any importance for him just then.

Ruff shrugged. "Let's go—it's that way."

They hurried toward the entrance, Ruff glancing back once to see Andy Farmer intently fusing his explosives. Even then he could hear them, hear them far below in the bowels of the ancient mountain. The groaning, whimpering sounds of their pursuers as they searched their way through the darkness—them, the ones who could not die. The Stone Warriors.

"My brother," Sarah said unhappily.

"You can't stop him."

"He must be m—"

"Yeah, he's mad. Seeing your father and the others get it did something to him. Maybe he's not crazy in the usual way, but as far as the Stone Warriors go, he's crazier than hell."

"And he can't stop."

"Not until they're all dead," Ruff said. They had reached the cavern mouth and were ready to start on down through the darkness. Sarah was close beside Ruff. Gertrude held Sarah's hand, following obediently, like a child. She was still in shock, quite willing to let someone else take the responsibility for thinking. Ruff stood Cobb on his feet and supported him.

Cobb wasn't that far gone. He held up abruptly and spun away. "We can't let him do this."

The wind whipped water into their faces, above them the dark bluff rose, and far below, the river snaked past.

"You haven't got any choice about it," Ruff said angrily.

"He's destroying it all. All." Cobb's fists were clenched before him. His hair was washed down into his face. "I won't allow it."

"If you try to stop him, he'll kill you too," Ruff guessed. "It's not worth it."

"But I—"

"I'm not waiting, dammit," Justice exploded. "I'm getting the hell off this mountain and I'm taking the women with me before something else can happen to them. We've got Stone Warriors behind us, possibly ahead of us, and the mountain charged with explosives. Back there a madman's waiting to light the fuse. You want to go talk to him?"

Cobb sagged, visibly sagged. He shook his head at the futility of it.

"Come on," Ruff said, and he started off, climbing down the jumbled rock slide toward the stony chute below, the women still holding hands, following as closely as possible. When Ruff glanced back, he saw the professor struggling to catch up.

They traveled along the bluffs for half a mile before dropping to the creek bed. There was nothing to be seen anywhere. The storm blacked out the world. They could hear the river, the wind, the patter of rain. Ruff thought the sky was graying slightly to the east. It was getting close to dawn.

When they all had caught their breath, they started on, along the streambed toward the juncture with the Little Mo two miles on. They were soaked through and exhausted when they reached it. The skies were paling. A flight of passenger pigeons swarmed by against the western horizon, going to feed before the rains returned.

"What do we do now?" Sarah asked. She was panting, leaning against Ruff, trying on a brave little smile that brightened her face considerably.

"Now we wait."

"If he was coming, he'd be here," Cobb objected.

"I told the kid I'd wait," Ruff said.

"He didn't make it. If he'd managed to get the fuse lit, we would have heard it go up. We'd have heard the dynamite, right?"

"Professor," Ruff Justice said wearily, "shut up."

They climbed the low sandy rise to sit in silence, watching dawn pierce the cloud cover here and there with silver arrows that danced on the river, watching a brief flurry of color—crimson and orange, bright gold—stain the high rain clouds before the grayness of day set in again.

When it went, it was with unexpected violence. Cobb

heard the rumbling and leapt to his feet. The ground trembled beneath them.

"Look," Cobb shouted.

A long finger pointed northward. The professor's face sagged with amazement. The bluffs that had sheltered the caves of the Stone Warriors quivered, the top lifting like a cake as fire spewed out of one entrance. The top lifted, seemed to hover momentarily, and then collapsed, collapsed with the damnedest boom, dust, smoke, and debris fountaining high into the morning sky.

"He did it," Cobb said, and there was actually a tear in his eye. "He blew them up. Blew them all up. Every trace of them. Damn it to hell!"

The bluffs still trembled. The top had just folded in, taking the walls with it. Ruff saw that the river, agitated by the following landslide, was running white now. He shook his head, looked for a long moment at the column of dust reaching cloudward, then turned away.

"We can go now," Cobb said.

"We're waiting," Justice replied.

"He's dead. He has to be. His madness killed him."

"We can wait." Ruff didn't argue anymore. He sat down, knees drawn up.

Sarah Farmer was beside him, her head resting on his shoulder. "Do you think he's alive?" she asked once.

"He'll come or he won't come."

"If he comes . . ." She hesitated. "Will he be any good after this? I mean . . ."

"I know what you mean. I don't know. Maybe he's gotten all the poison out of his system." Maybe. The dust still hung in the air, forming a flat, dirty cloud.

"Someone's coming," Cobb said excitedly.

Ruff was on his feet in a single catlike movement, his eyes narrowing. No one had any guarantee that there were no more Stone Warriors, that they had all been inside the caves.

"Horses," Justice said in puzzlement.

"Keep and Hallop?"

"I can't tell."

"There's only one rider—three horses," Sarah said, her voice rising with excitement. "Oh, Ruff, it is! It is him! Gertrude, it's my brother."

Gertrude Eccles, who had drifted off into her own private misty world, apparently couldn't have cared less. Ruff put his arm around Sarah, feeling her eagerness, the sheer joy in the woman.

They could see him clearly now. Andy Farmer riding along the sandy wash astride a roan horse—Cobb's horse—leading two other animals. A bay and a strapping black with one ear daubed white.

That alone was enough to lift Ruff's spirits. He hadn't thought much of the idea of crossing the plains afoot with the Sioux roaming the area.

They walked to the edge of the rise en masse and waited for Farmer. As he drew nearer, they got a truly fantastic picture of a man who has been through hell and learned to like it.

Farmer's clothes were rags, burned, blackened. His hair was singed off short like someone had stuck him headfirst into a campfire. His eyebrows were gone, as was that wisp of a beard. His face was black, lumpy on one side. And he was laughing like a maniac, laughing and cheering, his white teeth brilliant behind fire-blackened lips.

"Got 'em! Got 'em, every last mother's son! Got 'em!" His voice rose to a piercing shriek that broke off hoarsely. He leapt from the roan's back and charged up the sandy slope to his sister, picking her up, spinning her around in his burned arms. "Killed 'em all! Killed 'em all. They'll never rise out of that tomb. Nothing could. Finally dead."

Then it went out of him. His grin softened to a tight little smile, which in turn faded away and left him standing there, a dirty young man who'd been through hell and still had a long way to come back.

"Where were the horses, Andy?"

It was a minute before Farmer seemed to hear Ruff's question. "They had the bunch of them in a little canyon. One was already gone."

"Gone?" Cobb asked querulously.

"They eat them, you know. Anyway, I got these three."

Ruff was looking over the horses. The black seemed glad to see him and nipped at his leg to prove it. Ruff swatted the muzzle away. His horse seemed perfectly sound, as did the others.

When the black tried to nip him again, Ruff growled, "You be good to me, son. At least I never wanted to make steaks out of you." Louder he called, "Let's move on out of here. I don't want to be in the badlands at dark."

"Neither do I," Sarah said with a shudder. "I don't want to see this country again—ever. Gold or no gold."

Cobb said he guessed he had nothing left to stay for, either, and they mounted up, Sarah and Ruff on the black, Cobb and Gertrude on the bay. Andy Farmer rode alone. It was a silent little party, silent and bleak. There was too much blood on the back trail.

"Just a minute," Andy Farmer said. "Ruff, I want to go south a way. That next canyon."

"All right. Any reason?"

"You'll see, I reckon," the kid answered, and Ruff shrugged.

They rode up the feeder canyon toward the rim where the red cedar grew. It took them an hour to go up five hundred feet to the rim. There they stood perspiring, looking out across the shadowed badlands, while Andy Farmer explored in the rocks above them.

"What's he doing?" Cobb demanded. No one answered him.

Andy circled the lightning-struck oak twice and then started digging, clearing out the head-sized boulders that clotted a narrow fissure. Ruff, watching him, saw him hoist the leather saddlebags fifteen minutes later. They were heavy, very heavy. Andy Farmer came back down the slope, knelt down on the ground before them, and opened the bags.

"All right. That's it. I wouldn't have cared, but Dad wanted Sarah to have things."

"It's gold?"

"That's right. Eleven sacks of dust. We hid ours. Tom Keep wouldn't." Farmer stared off into space. "That seems far back, in a different life."

"Is that much?" Sarah asked, nodding toward the gold. "Enough to start a little shop or buy a home for Andy and me?"

She really didn't know, so Ruff told her. "It's enough, Sarah, enough to live the rest of your life on if you're careful with it."

"Can we go on?" The voice was Gertrude Eccles'. They were the first she had spoken in hours. The woman scientist looked very small, exhausted. "I'm tired of this place. Can we go on? I want to go home."

# 16

---◦◦▬◦◦---

They hit Lode at sundown, dragging down the main street as the saloons of the tiny mining town came to life and the lamps went on. The horses were weary, even the big black. It had been a long trail without food coming on top of days of exhausting labor and nervous tension.

"How beautiful it looks," Sarah said. "How grubby and horrible and filthy it looked on the way out, and how beautiful it seems now."

That was probably the only time in its existence Lode had received such a compliment. Ruff knew what she meant. He was happy to see the place himself, and as a rule, he despised towns. Towns are an outgrowth of civilization thrown up to provide mutual security, but there's no true security. The closer folks lived together, the more they needed to respect each other's rights, and the less they seemed to.

"Where to?" Andy asked. He looked around dubiously, like a wild thing come to a frightening place of captivity. His scorched face was blistered, puffed, savage in the meager lamplight.

"The hotel, of course," Sarah said brightly. "A be
and a bath. And a huge meal. Right, Ruff?"

"That's right. You folks go on ahead. Andy and
have a little errand to do."

Andy blinked twice at Ruff and shrugged. The
escorted the others to the hotel, which seemed sur
prised to have real women checking in, but otherwis
seemed clean and safe. Then Justice and Andy Farme
walked up the street to the nearest saloon, leadin
their horses.

"Am I slow, Justice? I don't get this."

"The gold, Andy. It's come this far, it'd be a sham
to lose it now." Ruff hitched his black. "Maybe you'
better wait out here."

"Sure." Andy still looked vaguely puzzled, but tha
wouldn't hurt him any.

Ruff went into the saloon, which was buzzing wit
meaningless talk and curses, the spin of a roulett
wheel, and the clicking of glass against glass. H
walked to the bar and waited until the bartender wa
free.

"Where's the local banker?"

"Pullen? Haven't seen him in here for weeks. He'
at the Grand, most likely. That's where the big shot
hang out."

"Thanks. Is he a Wells Fargo agent too?"

"Aren't they usually?"

"That's what I thought. Thanks."

Outside, it was raining again from out of a cold sky
Ruff led Andy Farmer toward the Grand Hotel an
Men's Club, a glorified saloon.

Harold T. Pullen was a thin, whining man wit
quick dark eyes. He was holding a lousy poker han
when Ruff Justice found him. "Do I know you, sir?" h
demanded.

"No. I've got something like twenty thousand i
dust outside that you might be familiar with, though.

"I'll fold," Pullen said hurriedly. He collected his chips and followed Justice out. They paraded over to the bank, where the dust was weighed and locked up. Andy Farmer took two hundred in cash money, the rest—something over seventeen thousand—in a draft on the Bismarck Wells Fargo.

That done, they returned to the hotel. Ruff was feeling gritty, tired of this long trail, which had meant so much pain to so many. He thought of facing MacEnroe and explaining about his contingent of cavalry, all wiped out, of explaining about the Stone Warriors.

"He's not going to like much of this," Ruff muttered.

"What?"

"Nothing, Andy. I'll stable the horses and meet you back here. Then we'll see how much food we can tuck away. The women will be washed and dressed and feeling better by then. They may want some new clothes. If so, I guess the storekeeper will open up for a man as prosperous as you."

Ruff led the horses off up the street. The rain was cold, light. There was someone following Ruff Justice. He wasn't very good at it, but he was trying his damnedest. He had been on Ruff's trail since they hit Lode. He had followed them to the bank and was sticking with Ruff. That meant it was Justice he wanted.

Ruff sighed and ground his teeth together. A man gets tired—tired of all of this foolishness, of all the killing. And that was what this man was setting himself up for.

The kid in the stable was gawky, sleepy, had one ear folded over. He made quite a fuss over the black, running respectful hands along its sleek flanks.

"Don't you worry, mister, don't you worry about this animal. I'll take care of him proper. Lord, that's a horse, ain't it?"

"It is that," Ruff said. He passed a silver dollar to the kid. "You got another way out of here?"

"Besides the front door?"

"That's right."

"I reckon, but there's a lot of junk and whatnot out the side. You'll have to walk through some mess."

"I'm light-footed," Ruff answered.

Justice went out the side door and across a littered yard. The night was cool and damp. Here and there a star broke through the high clouds.

When he reached the main street again, he was alone, or seemed to be. Either he had lost his tail or he was falling victim to imagination. There was no one around—no one that he knew, at least.

The others were in the hotel dining room. They made an odd little group. Cobb was by himself, morose, angry. Gertrude hadn't quite come to earth yet. She had on a cotton dress about three sizes too large and had a ribbon in her light-brown hair. Andy . . . well, Andy looked like the man shot from a cannon. Sarah had had him slick his hair down, but it hadn't helped much.

"Ruff."

"Hello, Sarah." He bent, kissed her cheek, and pulled up a chair.

"I was worried—I don't know why. I had a premonition of danger."

"Lay off those premonitions," Ruff said, laughing, "we've had all the trouble we can handle lately."

"Andy told me about the money. I wasn't thinking clearly enough to do that myself. Thank you."

She thanked him again later on. When they lay in her hotel bed side by side, her soft breast against his rib cage, her lips running along his jawline as her hand rested between his legs, lightly encouraging.

"You're a nice man, Ruff Justice."

"You sure of that?"

"Sure enough. You should hear the stories they tell about you, though. Before we hired you—well, I'd heard them all, and they were truly terrible."

"Who was telling them?"

Ruff's hand ran along Sarah's silky flank, down along the dip of her waist and up to her breast. He bent his head and kissed the nipple softly, feeling her shudder a little, feeling her grip tighten.

"Why, Mr. Keep, mostly. Keep and that nasty Regis Cavanaugh." Their lips met, and for a moment neither of them spoke as Sarah rolled onto her back to look up at him with starlit eyes, her knees slowly lifting and parting.

"Yes, he is a nasty fellow, isn't he?"

"I'm glad he's gone."

"And who says he is?" Ruff asked.

"Cavanaugh? Why, I thought . . . Oh, if Andy wasn't sniping at us, then it had to be Cavanaugh."

"I think so."

Ruff was to her, coming forward on hands and knees to look down at her soft beauty before going down, his chest touching her full breasts, his thighs grazing hers as he lay between her legs, feeling their clutch and quiver, feeling the warm excitement of her body as her fingers lifted his shaft and gently guided it into her, her nostrils flaring, her eyes wide, mouth slack.

He sank slowly into her, taking her warm comfort, letting her lips search his body, her hands grip his buttocks as she lifted herself against him.

There was no conversation, no other thought as their bodies fell into a common rhythm, rising and falling, Ruff guiding Sarah expertly through a world of sensuous joy, as he opened her and filled her, clung to her, stroked her gently, and then stirred her with whispered words, with tiny kisses and scoring nips. Her legs lifted higher and then locked behind his back as she held him prisoner to the wild excitement that was growing within her. She made small birdlike noises deep in her throat, small exhalations of effort with each stroke until the joy began to build in her throat, to flood her breasts and groin, and her efforts became spasmic, uncontrollable, a wild driving force deep within her whipping her on until her body was slick with perspiration as it worked against Ruff's, her fingers clutching at his solid shaft, cupping his sack as he lay pressed against her. And she suddenly came undone, shuddering, trembling as Ruff reached his own hard climax.

Neither spoke for fifteen minutes. Sarah made small cooing noises and covered him with steaming kisses. The night was cold, but together they were warm and perfect.

"He must hate you a lot," she said finally.

"Who?" Ruff muttered into the hollow of her shoulder. He had been ready to drift off into a deep, completely contented sleep.

"Regis Cavanaugh."

Ruff yawned. "No more'n he hates a hundred other people—including some he hasn't yet met. He's that kind of a man."

"Then why . . . ? He followed us all the way into the badlands. Or are you telling me it was Andy who was sniping?" The hand that had been stroking Ruff's back stopped its motion.

"No. No, it wasn't Andy. I think it was Regis Cavanaugh. But you see, the way he went about it was madness. A man has to be more than angry to follow us across the plains and into the badlands; Regis Cavanaugh was more than angry, more than mad."

"I don't understand . . ."

"He was being paid. Paid to kill us one by one."

"To kill every single member of our party?"

"That's what I believe. The blame could be placed

on the Indians, or better yet the Stone Warriors. Then the army could go there in force and finish off the bunch of them. And there would be no one left with a claim to the gold but . . ."

"Gregory Keep," Sarah said with sudden excitement.

"Had to be. He was the one who hired Cavanaugh. Why else hire a killer? He was the only one with us who had a claim to that gold. As the man said, gold makes us mad indeed."

"I suppose you're right," Sarah said quietly. "Though I hate to think anyone could be that cold-blooded. And Keep himself is dead now."

"Is he?"

"Well, I mean, he must be, mustn't he?"

"Why?"

"Well, we never saw him again after . . . No, he doesn't have to be dead at all, does he?"

"No, ma'am."

"But he won't . . . Is this all over, Ruff? I don't think I could take much more of it, honestly. It has to be all over."

"It is," he said. "It's all over." He told her that twice more, knowing each time that he was lying.

They were up with the dawn, and for the first time in many days the skies were mostly clear, just a few ragged, orange-edged clouds low on the western horizon marring the soft, empty distances. They could hear the sounds of the stamp mills, the ore crushers at work high on the hills as the miners tramped off to work. None of them felt he was missing anything by pulling out of Lode.

Cobb was considerably brighter that morning. He had decided that even without substantiating evidence he had enough information to write a startling, career-lifting paper. Dr. Eccles was somewhat recovered. Sarah was bright-eyed and shiny. Ruff had trouble keeping his eyes off her.

"Let's go and be damned to this place," Andy Farmer said. He had about the same opinion of Lode as Ruff Justice did.

"I'm ready. Sarah?"

"Yes."

He took her hand, squeezed it, and helped her up onto the buggy purchased that morning to sit beside Gertrude Eccles. Sarah had a new yellow dress, a yellow bonnet, and she was refreshing, beautiful in the morning light. As pretty as woman ever was, Ruff thought.

"Justice?"

Ruff turned.

Andy was just watching him. "Are we going to go or are you going to stand lookin' at her all morning?"

"I'd prefer the latter," Justice answered honestly, "but let's shake the dust off our feet. Lead on out."

Ruff walked to the big black and swung aboard. The sun was bright through the cottonwoods that lined the ribbonlike creek behind the stable. Andy Farmer was already crossing the stream, Cobb behind him, the buggy next.

Justice still held back the impatient black, taking one last uneasy glance around. He could see no one, but he was unhappy with things. There had been someone following him around Lode last evening, and he could think of only a few men who would want to do something like that—and none of them were friends.

He heeled the black forward, splashed across the creek, the water lifting from the horse's hooves in silver fans. The black was trembling with excitement, wanting to be out on the long-grass plains, running with the wind, wild and free as its ancestors had been.

They made good time that day. The long grass was wet, but the earth beneath it was firm. The flat plains were no place for a sniper, but Ruff was wary and he rode with both eyes open, sweeping far south and then north of the small party, searching the deep, suddenly gaping coulees, finding—thankfully—no one.

"Tomorrow," Cobb said that evening as they sat around a tiny flickering fire. "Tomorrow Bismarck and on east—and none too soon. I've had enough of the West, far too much."

"I haven't," Sarah Farmer said softly. Her eyes lifted to the man in buckskins who sat across from her, then lowered again.

"We're stayin', aren't we, Sarah?" Andy Farmer asked. "I was plannin' on goin' back and panning a little. I thought maybe you'd stay on."

"No. It's no place for me. You take over the claim, all of it."

"That's very generous of you, Miss Farmer," the voice from the edge of the camp said. "Considering the claim's not yours to begin with."

Ruff froze, cursing himself inwardly. He had blown it, blown it at the last minute.

"You just sit tight, Justice. You too, boy!" Gregory Keep came forward then, his pistol leveled. There were three men with him, men Ruff had never seen before—hired in Lode, no doubt. All of them were armed and all of them looked ready to do whatever needed to be done. There wasn't much doubt in Ruff's mind what Keep thought needed to be done on this night.

"Throw your guns over into the fire, Justice. You, too, kid. Who is that, Andy Farmer?"

"That's right."

"Justice, you're not moving fast enough. Shuck that damned Colt."

"Where's Rupert Hallop? Did he make it out?"

"Hallop's layin' back there with the soldier boys. I took care of them."

"Why Hallop? I thought he was your man."

"Did you? So did I. You know who he was? His

name was Art MacDonald. MacDonald! Heard that name before?"

"One of the other partners."

"That's right. Hallop was tagging along trying to keep an eye on his own stake. He crossed me. Balked at killing that corporal, so I got him too." He was into the firelight now, standing over Ruff, his whiskered face dark and hungry. The fox was completely gone now. Only the wolf, the killing wolf was left of Gregory Keep. "Toss that Colt, Justice. Now!"

Ruff didn't like this setup. He didn't like turning his gun over to anyone. Not when he knew, knew that they were going to be killed anyway. He wanted to go out scrapping, if he had to go. Still, he might not have drawn against four men, fearing Sarah's safety, but the woman herself began things.

She had been carrying that little Remington .41 in her petticoats since the badlands, and now she decided to use it. She up and drew it, the little pop sounding deceptively innocent until Ruff, turning his head, saw that Gregory Keep had taken lead in the throat and he was falling, buckling at the knees, his pistol discharging into the campfire, spraying sparks.

The three hired guns were thrown into confusion. They had been prepared to throw down on women, kill them perhaps, but not to fight armed men. They hesitated and then they were lost.

Ruff drew, fired from his knee—left, then right— saw two men tagged hard, heard the roar of Andy's Winchester near at hand, and saw the third man shot dead. The man stood gaping at the bullet hole in his chest, nodded amiably at Justice, and then fell forward into the fire to snuff it.

And that was that. "It looks," Ruff said, "as if you've got a clear claim, lady."

She rushed across the camp and into his arms, and

Ruff stood there grinning, stroking her sleek, soft hair as she kissed him and whispered love words.

It was high noon when they reached Bismarck. The town was busy, the freight wagons rumbling through town, the saloons churning out tinkly music. No one paid any attention to the small party that drew up before the International House, their journey over at last, the dead buried, mourned for, soon to be forgotten.

They went inside together, asked for and got four rooms with tubs.

"I'm going to soak for days," Sarah said.

"Sounds like an idea."

"You can wash my back."

"Sounds like a better idea."

"I haven't gotten to my best ideas yet."

Ruff grinned. "You go ahead and have that bath, Sarah. A bath and a rest."

"You're going somewhere?"

"Out to the fort. The colonel likes to have me report promptly. But I'll be back. I'll get my town suit on and we'll massacre a couple of steaks. Then, later, we can get to some of your best ideas. Sound good?"

"It sounds, Mr. Justice, like the nicest offer I've ever had."

Colonel MacEnroe sat behind his desk at Fort Abraham Lincoln, his scowl deepening with each sentence Ruff spoke. "All gone," MacEnroe repeated several times. He was plain angry as he always was when he lost men. "All gone. Corporal Duggs and six men."

"I'm sorry," was all Ruff could say to that. He had a little of that guilt that comes from being alive when other, perhaps better, men have gone.

"Well," the colonel said heavily, rising, "I suppose you did all you could under the circumstances, Ruff. I know you thought this smelled funny from the start.

What did we gain? Gold for two civilians, a smattering of scientific knowledge for a couple of professors."

"It's more than we often gain, sir," Ruff pointed out. And it was true; most times men died for nothing at all out here.

"I'm going to have a drink, Ruffin," MacEnroe said. "And then I believe I'll have another. Would you like to watch me?"

"No, sir." Ruff got to his feet as well. "I've a date with a friend."

"I see." MacEnroe nodded abstractedly. He was still thinking about his dead men. He was a good CO, was MacEnroe.

Ruff left him and crossed the parade ground, feeling a little gloomy himself. As he started changing into his dark town suit, a ruffled shirt underneath and black hat on his head, his spirits started to improve. He had begun thinking of what lay ahead now, not of what he had left behind.

It was dusk when Ruff came out of the barracks, looked to the purple-streaked skies, mounted the big black, and headed for Bismarck through the gathering shadows.

The river rolled past darkly; Bismarck was lighting up. The skies were filmed with purple, touched here and there with scarlet fire. Birds chattered in the willows along the Missouri.

Ruff yawned, lifted his arms to stretch, and was sledgehammered from the saddle, the report of the rifle following hours later, years later, echoing in his ears as he fell to the earth and the black danced away in fright. It took hours to hit the ground, but when he hit it, the impact was terrific. The breath was driven from his lungs.

*Cavanaugh.*

He knew instantly what had happened, who it was, and he tried reaching for his holstered town gun, *tried*, and tried again. The hand wouldn't respond. The bullet had grazed Ruff's skull. He could feel the blood trickling into his left eye as he lay on his face in the river mud. He tried to blink away the blood, blink away the blinding pain, the confusion.

*The gun, dammit!*

The cool, deep-blue little Colt New Line .41 riding in its shoulder holster. It wasn't a lot of gun, but it was something—a hope, a chance. Ruff could see his fingers now creeping toward his shoulder holster, futile little white worms, working slowly. It was coming back, slowly. The feeling was coming back in his hand, his thoughts were clearing. Slowly.

He could hear the horse approaching now, being ridden at a flat-out run, the stirrups slapping against the animal's flanks. The sky was growing dark and the man was coming. Ruff willed that hand to move, cursed it, pleaded with it, but nothing would speed its slow progress.

He touched the butt of the little Colt. He was actually touching it. And coming on the run was Regis Cavanaugh, swinging down from his horse before it had stopped, rushing toward Ruff Justice, the long rifle going to his shoulder. The long rifle that had killed so many men.

Ruff could see the malicious glint in Cavanaugh's eye as he peered down the sights, and then he saw nothing. The .41 swung up, coming to sudden life, and Ruff touched off, the bullet burying itself in Cavanaugh's face, shattering nose and cranial bone on its way to the rancid little brain behind the dark eyes.

Cavanaugh's rifle boomed in answer, kicking mud up into Ruff's face as the bullet missed by a dozen inches.

Ruff slowly lowered his pistol and lay there for a long minute, letting it all come back. Regis Cavanaugh lay still and dead, watching with one darkly gleaming eye.

When Ruff felt strong enough to try it, he heaved himself to his feet. He stood wobbling, the pistol dangling from his hand, staring down at Regis Cavanaugh.

Then he shook his head, turning away to walk after his horse. His town suit, he reflected, was ruined. It looked, Ruff thought, as if they were going to have to skip dinner altogether. A man can't go out to eat in a torn and muddy suit. They'd just have to skip that and get on to some of those other ideas Sarah seemed to have.

Ruff caught up the black's reins, swung aboard, and sat there for a moment, watching the river run. Then he shucked his dirty coat, balled it up, and threw it away. The tie followed.

Then he heeled the black forward toward Bismarck, whistling as he rode, and the river rambled away to the southern lands.

## WESTWARD HO!

**The following is the opening section from the next novel in the gun-blazing, action-packed new Ruff Justice series from Signet:**
**RUFF JUSTICE #15: CHEYENNE MOON**

Barton McGinnis hailed the gold camp again, but there was no answer. He didn't like the look of things, didn't like the feeling crawling up his spine.

McGinnis had spent the better part of his adult life on the Dakota plains. He had hunted the big herds and tried his hand at prospecting. He had wintered out along the Heart River when there wasn't a white man within a hundred miles, when the Sioux still were astonished to see a thunder gun, when it was no rare thing to go a year without seeing another man of any kind. Barton McGinnis had married and shed three different Indian wives. He had taken a grizzly bear with nothing but his bowie knife (paid the price of one eye and three fingers for that bit of work), lost most of one ear to frostbite and been punctured with arrows so many times that he felt close kin to the porcupine.

A man has to have a certain sort of sixth sense to endure that kind of life. Barton McGinnis believed he had it. If he did, it was aching now.

He started walking his gray horse down the long sandy bluff which faced the shallow, rapidly flowing

Heart River. The willows shifted in the wind, which
blew down from the north. It was a gray and dreary
day.

And something was damn sure wrong.

McGinnis held his horse up. He slipped the cover
from his repeating rifle and sat staring at the gold
camp, unable to make sense out of it.

"Hello the camp!" he tried again, but there was still
no answer. The horses grazed off to one side. They had
been hobbled and there they still stood, tails turned to
the wind. Well—it wasn't Indians then. Not if they
still had their horses.

"What in hell?" Barton now noticed the tracks for
the first time.

A single unshod pony had crossed the river here. It
had, in fact, crossed the river at least a dozen times.
Barton looked warily toward the willow brush which
fronted the Heart, looked again to the camp and shook
his head, not liking the smell of this at all.

The rider, whoever it was, had crossed and recrossed
the river at this point. Always in the same direction,
meaning that he was riding in circles.

"What for?" Barton asked the empty day. His horse's
ears twitched. "What for does someone ride around in
circles? Around an empty camp."

A camp that the week before had held sixteen miners,
all hopefully panning the Heart and the Little Heart.
Green, most of them were, but they had had Tug
Gates with them and Tug knew the land. They hadn't
struck much paydirt yet when Barton had seen them
last, and Barton had been inclined to think they
wouldn't.

He had shared their fire, wished them well and
headed up into the foothills where Little Jack, the
Shoshone, had told him there was a good-sized herd of
wild horses. He hadn't had much luck with the horses.

It seemed the prospectors had had even less luck.

Barton McGinnis crossed the Heart River, the water going to his tall gray's belly. He didn't like this, didn't like it a bit. That extra sense of his was raising pure hell.

"Hello the camp!" he tried again.

"You just turn around and get the hell out of here before I blow you from the saddle!" a savage but weak-sounding voice said from the screen of willows.

"Just a minute, friend," McGinnis replied, "what's going on here? Where's everyone? Where's Tug Gates?"

"McGinnis?" There was a moment's uncertain hesitation. "Is that you, McGinnis?"

"Damn right it's me. Who the hell did you think it was," Barton said angrily, for he recognized the voice now despite the strange quality it carried. Tug Gates had gotten almighty shy.

"I didn't know. I couldn't tell . . . come on in, Bart. For God's sake, I'm glad you came back! I'm glad it's you."

Barton's frown deepened and he walked the gray up through the willow brush toward the camp. What in the hell was the matter with Tug? And *where* was everyone else?

Barton knew who was waiting for him, but all the same he approached very slowly, his single eye darting from side to side, endlessly searching. The hoofprints of the other horse were clearly defined in the mud near the river. Circling—endlessly circling. Barton shook his head.

"Tug?" he called out. "Where are you?"

There was no answer. The willows rustled in the wind and the river rambled past. Barton McGinnis's horse shifted its feet and blew.

The sound which reached Barton's ears was scarcely human. Low, moaning, agonized, it lifted above the wind for a moment and then died away again.

"Tug?"

Barton's eyes narrowed. He cocked the Henry re
peater he carried and started his gray toward th
sound. He found Tug fifty feet on.

"God damnit," Barton said, his mouth twisting u
with revulsion. There wasn't much left of Tug Gates
The prospector lay on his side, wearing a twill coat
out at the elbows, homespun pants and a white collar
less shirt. All of his clothes were smeared with blood

Barton swung down, looking around cautiously a
he moved to Tug Gates, seeing the grooves Tug ha
carved into the sand getting where he was.

They had broken his legs for him and he had dragge
himself a long way to find cover. Barton recognize
the leg wounds for what they were—Tug had bee
trampled by a horse, deliberately trampled. Barto
thought of the unknown rider, the circling rider, bu
he couldn't make anything out of that. He walked t
his saddle, got his canteen and bedroll and tried mak
ing Tug comfortable.

Tug Gates was in bad shape, very bad. He would b
lucky if he lasted the night. He kept trying to talk
but Barton couldn't make much out of what he wa
saying.

He propped Tug up and tucked the blanket aroun
him. He was shivering badly but Barton had no incli
nation to start a fire for any reason whatsoever—no
until he understood what had been happening here
Tug's babbling didn't help.

". . . In a circle. You know," he moaned. Then hi
fingers clutched Barton's wrist with amazing strength
His eyes went wide, looking past Barton, into th
distance where his memory was reconstructing th
episode.

"Where's everyone else, Tug? Dead, alive? What'
happened? Was it the Indians done this?"

"Around in a circle you know and then the heads al
skinned . . . you know."

Barton said he knew. He didn't. He didn't know a damn thing and talking to Tug wasn't helping much. Barton tried again.

"The others, Tug. Fifteen men, Tug. Where in hell are they?"

"Over there." Tug's head rolled toward Barton. His teeth chattered violently now. It took him a time to stammer out the words, "You can see them over there. All in a row."

Tug's hand lifted and Barton McGinnis followed the broken, bloodied finger the dying man raised. He turned and walked through the brush and into the prospecting camp. He saw dead fire rings, two pitched tents, the hobbled horses, eyeing him warily. A lean-to sheltering picks and shovels, a few bedrolls stacked together, others laid out as if someone were preparing to climb in.

No one would be doing that. Barton McGinnis found the missing men. Or part of them.

There were fifteen stakes driven into the ground at intervals, forming a circle thirty feet in circumference. There were lines drawn in the sand like the spokes of a wheel from one stake to another.

On each stake a fleshless skull had been placed.

Barton McGinnis had to turn away. He wasn't sick, but he came damn close. Fifteen men! He went nearer, the skulls staring at him, the wind whistling, chanting in the trees.

McGinnis crouched down and examined a skull. Fresh. The skin peeled off of it. The jaw was missing. A cross had been drawn on the forehead with charcoal.

"Damn it all." Barton stood and looked back toward the river. He didn't believe in spooks and specters, in devils and moaning, creeping things—but this was enough to get the better of anyone.

"What does it mean?" That bothered him. He'd never seen anything like it, and McGinnis had seen some things on the plains and in the hills. He walked a slow circle, seeing that each skull had been positioned the same, facing the center of the wheel. Each had a smudged cross on it. Outside of that there was nothing to be learned. There were no corpses, no guns, no signs of battle, nothing.

"Only Tug knows now," McGinnis said. "Only Tug and he's not going to know anything for much longer."

Barton crossed the camp but he found nothing else. Gold-panning equipment lay in the river. In one bedroll he found a sack of dust. And of course there were the hoofprints.

"And what, damn me, does that mean?" McGinnis asked the empty day. Those tracks he had seen across the river ran in a circle around the camp. The distance was something like a hundred and fifty feet out from the center of the camp. It was a while before it hit Barton—

The horse had circled the camp fifteen times.

"Jesus," McGinnis muttered. He walked rather rapidly back to where Tug still lay. "I hope to hell you're gone, Tug. Sorry, old timer, but I hope you've faded away. Because I want nothing more right now than to get the hell out of here."

McGinnis didn't get that break. Tug was still holding on when the plainsman got back to the shelter of the willows. Barton hunkered down to touch Tug's forehead, to offer him a meaningless smile. Tug looked up at the one-eyed man and tried to say something which didn't come out.

"I won't leave you," McGinnis said, guessing at his meaning. "Whoever it was, they won't get you. I'll set watch."

There wasn't much else to do. McGinnis wasn't going to leave the man—he wasn't made that way—and Tug Gates wasn't fit to travel, smashed up the way he was. Tug hung on and McGinnis crouched beside him, feeling guilty about wishing Tug would kick off. The gold camp was spooky, oppressive. McGinnis was gripping his rifle a lot tighter than he needed to.

The sun was already low in the western sky, coasting toward the broken, rugged hills beyond the Heart, and McGinnis was getting edgy. He sure as hell didn't want to be out here at night. He wished he had a bottle of whiskey, he wished Tug would cash in his chips, wished Little Jack hadn't spotted those wild horses.

The shadows were long beneath the willows. Lengthening, they crossed and intermingled, turning to pools of darkness. The hills were deep in shadow and an owl hooted somewhere. There was still color in the western sky but there wouldn't be for long.

"I want a drink," Tug Gates said quite distinctly. He lifted his head and peered at McGinnis. "I want a drink of water, Bart."

"Sure."

"I'm sorry about this, Bart."

"Don't think a thing about it." There wasn't much water in the canteen. McGinnis propped up Tug's head and poured. Most of it missed the man's mouth. McGinnis patiently tried again. There wasn't enough water to wet his lips. "Hold on, I'll fill it."

Barton rose and walked to the river. He dipped the canteen in the Heart and crouched, waiting for it to fill. A second later he came leaping to his feet, nearly stumbling in sheer amazement.

The horse! There was a horse splashing across the river, being ridden in a lazy circle around the camp. The rider came on and Barton McGinnis, experienced as he was, stood mesmerized, knowing his rifle was back with Tug, knowing he needed it—now!

Still he couldn't move, couldn't force his mind to accept what the eyes saw.

The horse was across the river now, swinging through

the willows, loping toward the camp. McGinnis took off at a dead run, long legs flying, arms windmilling. The canteen floated away downstream.

"It was a woman, was what it was," McGinnis told himself over and over. "A woman. A dark haired woman. Just a woman."

And she hadn't been wearing a shirt.

She had come riding in a slow circle, mounted on a dark horse, dark hair blowing out behind her. Indian? She must have been, but McGinnis wouldn't have sworn to it. It was like nothing he had ever seen—all of this was unreal and she was just the topper. A woman, a young and nicely built one without anything on above the waist riding lazily around that camp, slowly making the sixteenth loop as if there wasn't a damn thing off about it . . .

McGinnis burst into the clearing and his stomach went cold with fear. His rifle was gone. Tug Gates was still there—but he didn't have a head.

McGinnis heard the horse crashing through the willows and he started running again, running for the river. He looked behind him and saw her plain as day. Young, beautiful, shirtless, a she-demon with savage eyes and in her hand was the head of Tug Gates.

McGinnis hit the river at a dead run, ripping off his shirt as the cold current clutched at him, swept him away. A rifle shot echoed across the water, and McGinnis saw the half-naked woman sitting on that dark horse, rifle to her shoulder. She fired again and McGinnis dove under, holding his breath as long as possible, holding it until he thought his lungs would burst, until he surfaced gasping, choking, his head spinning, far downstream.

There was only a single rose-colored pennant of cloud high in the sky. The rest of the world was dark, comfortingly dark. The river rambled away and Baron McGinnis rode the current, not looking back, not wanting to see anything of her or of the gold camp. He rode the river away and the night things shrieked their mockery from the wilderness shore.

# JOIN THE RUFF JUSTICE READERS' PANEL

Help us bring you more of the books you like by filling out thi survey and mailing it in today.

1. Book title:_____

   Book #:_____

2. Using the scale below how would you rate this book on the following features.

| Poor | | Not so Good | | | O.K. | | | Good | | Excellent |
|---|---|---|---|---|---|---|---|---|---|---|
| 0 | 1 | 2 | 3 | 4 | 5 | 6 | 7 | 8 | 9 | 1 |

|  | Rating |
|---|---|
| Overall opinion of book....................... | ___ |
| Plot/Story............................... | ___ |
| Setting/Location........................... | ___ |
| Writing Style............................. | ___ |
| Character Development...................... | ___ |
| Conclusion/Ending......................... | ___ |
| Scene on Front Cover....................... | ___ |

3. On average about how many western books do you buy fo

   yourself each month?_____

4. How would you classify yourself as a reader of westerns?
   I am a ( ) light ( ) medium ( ) heavy reader.

5. What is your education?
   ( ) High School (or less)      ( ) 4 yrs. college
   ( ) 2 yrs. college             ( ) Post Graduate

6. Age_____      7. Sex: ( ) Male ( ) Female

Please Print Name_____

Address_____

City_____State_____Zip_____

Phone # (        )_____

Thank you. Please send to New American Library, Researc Dept, 1633 Broadway, New York, NY 10019.

## Exciting Westerns by Jon Sharpe

(0451)

- [ ] THE TRAILSMAN #19: SPOON RIVER STUD (123875—$2.50)*
- [ ] THE TRAILSMAN #20: THE JUDAS KILLER (124545—$2.50)*
- [ ] THE TRAILSMAN #21: THE WHISKEY GUNS (124898—$2.50)*
- [ ] THE TRAILSMAN #22: BORDER ARROWS (125207—$2.50)*
- [ ] THE TRAILSMAN #23: THE COMSTOCK KILLERS (125681—$2.50)*
- [ ] THE TRAILSMAN #24: TWISTED NOOSE (126203—$2.50)*
- [ ] THE TRAILSMAN #25: MAVERICK MAIDEN (126858—$2.50)*
- [ ] THE TRAILSMAN #26: WARPAINT RIFLES (127757—$2.50)*
- [ ] THE TRAILSMAN #27: BLOODY HERITAGE (128222—$2.50)*
- [ ] THE TRAILSMAN #28: HOSTAGE TRAIL (128761—$2.50)*

*Price is $2.95 in Canada

**Buy them at your local
bookstore or use coupon
on next page for ordering.**

## Exciting Westerns by Jon Sharpe from SIGNET

(0451)

☐ THE TRAILSMAN #1: SEVEN WAGONS WEST (127293—$2.50)*
☐ THE TRAILSMAN #2: THE HANGING TRAIL (110536—$2.25)
☐ THE TRAILSMAN #3: MOUNTAIN MAN KILL (121007—$2.50)*
☐ THE TRAILSMAN #4: THE SUNDOWN SEARCHERS (122003—$2.50)*
☐ THE TRAILSMAN #5: THE RIVER RAIDERS (127188—$2.50)*
☐ THE TRAILSMAN #6: DAKOTA WILD (119886—$2.50)*
☐ THE TRAILSMAN #7: WOLF COUNTRY (123697—$2.50)
☐ THE TRAILSMAN #8: SIX-GUN DRIVE (121724—$2.50)*
☐ THE TRAILSMAN #9: DEAD MAN'S SADDLE (126629—$2.50)*
☐ THE TRAILSMAN #10: SLAVE HUNTER (114655—$2.25)
☐ THE TRAILSMAN #11: MONTANA MAIDEN (116321—$2.25)
☐ THE TRAILSMAN #12: CONDOR PASS (118375—$2.50)*
☐ THE TRAILSMAN #13: BLOOD CHASE (119274—$2.50)*
☐ THE TRAILSMAN #14: ARROWHEAD TERRITORY (120809—$2.50)*
☐ THE TRAILSMAN #15: THE STALKING HORSE (121430—$2.50)*
☐ THE TRAILSMAN #16: SAVAGE SHOWDOWN (122496—$2.50)*
☐ THE TRAILSMAN #17: RIDE THE WILD SHADOW (122801—$2.50)*
☐ THE TRAILSMAN #18: CRY THE CHEYENNE (123433—$2.50)*

*Price is $2.95 in Canada

Buy them at your local bookstore or use this convenient coupon for ordering.

NEW AMERICAN LIBRARY,
P.O. Box 999, Bergenfield, New Jersey 07621
Please send me the books I have checked above. I am enclosing $_____
(please add $1.00 to this order to cover postage and handling). Send check
or money order—no cash or C.O.D.'s. Prices and numbers are subject to change
without notice.

Name _____
Address_____
City_____ State_____ Zip Code_____
Allow 4-6 weeks for delivery.
This offer is subject to withdrawal without notice.